JACKAL & HIDE

A KENYA KANGA MYSTERY

VICTORIA TAIT

KANGA
PRESS

Dedication
Cynthia Gould
For her Help, Advice & Encouragement

STYLE & KISWAHILI GLOSSARY

The main character, Mama Rose, has a British upbringing and she uses British phrases.

Kiswahili words are used to add to the richness and authenticity of the setting and characters, and most are linked to this Glossary.

- *Amref* Kenyan medics and flying doctor service
- *Asante* Thank you
- *Askari* Watchman / Security Guard
- *Ayah* Kenyan nanny
- *Bahati Njema* Good Luck
- *BATUK* British Army Training Unit Kenya

- *Boda Boda* Motorbike used as a taxi
- *Bwana* Sir, a term of respect used for an older man
- Chai Tea made by boiling leaves/tea bag with milk (and sugar).
- *Habari* Greeting used like hello but meaning 'What news?'
- *Habari Yako?* How are you?
- *Hapana* No
- *Kanga* Colourful cotton fabric (also Swahili for guinea fowl)
- *Kikoi* Brightly coloured cotton garment or sarong
- *Kikuyu* Kenyan ethnic group or tribe
- *Kongoi* 'Thank you' in Kipsigis dialect
- *KSPCA* Kenya Society for the Protection & Care of Animals
- *KWS* Kenya Wildlife Service
- *NSSF* National Insurance and Pension State Fund
- *Memsaab* Madam
- *Muram* Gravel road
- *Mzuri* Good
- *Mzuri Sana* Very Good
- *Mzungu* European/White person
- *Pole* Sorry (Pronounced Pow-lay)
- *Safari Njeme* Have a good journey

- *Safari Salama* I wish you a safe journey
- *Samosa* Fried pastry with savoury filling
- *Sawa (sawa)* Fine, all good, no worries.
- *Shamba* Vegetable patch/garden (or farm)
- *Siafu* Driver/Fire ants with a very painful bite
- *Shuka* Thin, brightly coloured blanket in bright checked colours, where red is often the dominant colour. Also used as a sarong or throw
- *Stoney Tangawizi Ginger Beer* - a popular brand of ginger beer.
- *Tafadhali* Please
- *Tusker* Popular Brand of Beer

OTHER TERMS

- *Car Park* Parking Lot
- *Grit* Small pieces of stone or gravel
- *Kerb* Curb
- *Torch* Flashlight

AUTHOR'S NOTE

In *Jackal & Hide*, many clues are laid before you and Mama Rose become aware that a murder has been committed. So please read carefully and see if you can work out the victim's identity, who the perpetrator is and, probably more importantly, how and why the crime is committed.

Mama Rose has many demands made upon her and she is rather distracted at the beginning of the story, but once the mystery starts, the pace increases and emotions run high.

I hope you enjoy *Jackal & Hide*.

PROLOGUE

The jackal emerged from its den and sniffed the air. The waning sun left a rim of orange on the horizon at the edge of the plain. The smell the jackal detected was human. There had been many of them over the past week disturbing the peace of Lewa Downs. But this was different. It smelt of... food.

The jackal trotted towards the source of the aroma but found its way blocked by the branches and spikes of an acacia bush. It skirted the bush and slid forward on its belly, avoiding the long protruding spikes of other white thorn acacia bushes.

It emerged into a small clearing and stood, alert to the sounds of other creatures. The smell was stronger now, but mingled with another scent, that of hyena. The jackal stiffened and cocked its head. It was alone, but still moved stealthily towards a clump of devil's horsewhip. Areas of the undergrowth had been trampled and there were tracks made by earlier animal visitors.

The jackal stopped and surveyed the dead body. It had already been attacked by hyenas, and they would soon return. Its attention was caught by the sparkle of a gold ring, reflecting the final strands of daylight. Grasping at the object, it found its supper was not attached to the body, so it closed its jaw firmly.

Hearing the snap of twigs and smelling the stink of hyena, it trotted away across the clearing, through a gap in the trees and out onto the open savannah, still grasping the left hand of a young woman firmly in its mouth.

CHAPTER ONE

R ose Hardie looked up from the email she was reading on her tablet and announced, "Chris is coming over from the UK for the Lewa Marathon."

Her husband Craig was dozing in his large cedar-wood chair on their outdoor patio. He jolted awake and opened his eyes, exclaiming, "What? Did you say Chris is running at Lewa?"

Rose, known to many locally as "Mama Rose", was sixty-five years old. She sat up on the wooden sofa she had been lying on and watched the clouds part to reveal the peak of Mount Kenya. The majestic mountain dominated the skyline of Nanyuki, the small Kenyan town where she lived, three hours north of the capital, Nairobi.

She smiled and said, "Apparently he has some old friends from his British army days who are serving here with BATUK. And they're short of a teammate, so they invited him to join them."

Craig, who was in his early seventies, crossed his arms. "Is he going to stay with us or with his pals?"

Craig and Chris had fallen out, and Rose had barely seen their son for the past fifteen years. When he had returned to Kenya less than two months ago, she had tried to rebuild the bridges between them, but it was apparent that Craig still felt some animosity towards Chris.

"Is Heather coming with him?" Craig's face softened as he mentioned their daughter's name.

Rose shook her head. "I don't think so, but I'm sure she's still planning to be here by the end of June. I mean the end of the month. Can you believe it's the first of June already? Where has the year gone?"

Craig struggled to sit up. She moved across to help him and rearranged the cushions which supported his back. Craig was finding it increasingly difficult to move by himself.

A secondary infection, a result of a childhood bout of polio, was slowly paralysing the left side of his body. On top of that, he had suffered a minor stroke, and Rose was concerned he was heading towards a full-blown one. His blood pressure remained high despite regular check-ups and beta-blocker medicine administered by Dr Farrukh.

Rose pulled a small stool across to Craig's chair and sat down next to him like a child. She picked up his hand and said, "You realise this could be last time you see Chris? Please don't antagonise him. I would really hate it if you two don't reconcile your differences."

Craig slowly turned his head and looked down at Rose. She thought she glimpsed a tear in the corner of his eye.

He admitted, "I know I've been hard on him. And I was annoyed when he didn't choose the path I thought he should. But he's a fine man, and he's served his country well. That is the UK, in the British Army. But I worry he won't be here to look after you when I'm gone."

She squeezed his hand. "You don't need to worry. We have our friends here, and they will keep an eye on me. And there's our staff, who are really like a family to me. Look at how well Samwell looked after you when I was away at the Rhino Charge event. And we can't forget Kipto."

"Mama," said a voice behind them.

Rose stood, stretched out her back, and faced Kipto, their housegirl of unknown age.

"Young Thabiti is here. With his dog," Kipto announced.

A small, fluffy, white shape raced around the corner and jumped up at Kipto.

"Shoo," she said, waving her arms, but she allowed the dog to follow her into the house.

Thabiti Onyango, a young African man, strolled around the corner of the house. He was dressed neatly in tan-coloured shorts and polo shirt, and wore his hair close-cropped, with a neat beard and moustache encircling his mouth.

"Habari," he greeted them. "I thought I'd pop over and see how you both are. And I wanted to quiz you about farming methods." He looked across at Craig. "The new lodge in Borana Conservancy, the one Marina is working at, is considering growing some of its own food using hydroponics. Borana already has a permaculture farm."

"Drinks?" Rose asked, and the two men nodded absent-mindedly as Thabiti squatted by Craig and opened a folder.

She watched them and felt a warmth in her chest. To think it was less than six months since Thabiti had lost his mother and she had helped him find her killer. Thabiti was growing in confidence and strengthening into a man, but he still displayed his boyhood anxieties.

She was delighted he had a project to occupy and interest him. And his relationship with Marina, an attractive and bubbly Indian girl from Nairobi, was blossoming. They had been offered work together to manage a private lodge for a family in Borana Conservancy. Marina had gone ahead to organise staff and set up the lodge before the family visited.

"How is Marina getting on?" she asked.

Thabiti swivelled on his heels and replied, "She's struggling a bit with the staff. I think she had to sack someone this week. But she'll be in town tomorrow interviewing other candidates and organising more supplies. She'll be in Dormans most of the morning if you want to meet her for coffee."

CHAPTER TWO

The following morning, Thursday, Rose and Craig were seated at the old wooden dining table on their covered patio. Rose dipped her spoon into a bowl of home-made granola, fruit and yogurt as Kipto walked out of the cottage holding Rose's ringing mobile phone at arm's length.

Rose read Julius's name on the display. He was the head warden at the Mount Kenya Animal Orphanage, which had recently been incorporated into the Mount Kenya Wildlife Conservancy.

"Habari, Mama Rose," said Julius in an excited voice. "Someone has left us two baby ostriches in a cardboard box."

"Really?" she exclaimed. "Do you know where they came from?"

"I do not know, but can you come and look at them? And advise us what to do. They appear very young to me."

Rose had promised to spend some time with Craig this morning, but she couldn't ignore Julius's request or neglect his young charges. She worked as a community vet, attending to the injuries and illnesses suffered by cats and dogs, wildlife, and larger farm animals in Nanyuki and the surrounding area.

Her official government-recognised title was a veterinary paraprofessional, and she was formally accountable to her friend, Dr Emma, the only qualified vet in Nanyuki.

Dr Emma preferred to treat smaller animals in her town centre pharmacy, which doubled up as an operating theatre and treatment room. She left Rose to administer to the needs of larger animals, those located outside Nanyuki and most of the wildlife cases.

Rose hesitated before responding to Julius. "Of course. I'll be with you as soon as I can."

She placed the phone on the table and looked at Craig.

"Trouble?" he asked as his shoulders slumped.

She realised that he was disappointed, expecting her to jump up and leave him to attend to whatever emergency had been conveyed by the phone call. She brightened and asked, "How do you fancy a trip to the animal orphanage? You haven't been there for ages and it would give us a chance to try out that wheelchair the Cottage Hospital has lent us."

Craig licked his lips in anticipation, but then frowned. "But you couldn't manage all that on your own, and it sounds as if you have patients to deal with."

She placed her elbow on the table and massaged her chin. "I could drive your old Subaru and then we could take Samwell with us to help you. I think the wheelchair should fit in the back. Anyway, it might be easier for you than climbing in and out of my old Defender."

Rose turned the ignition key, and despite not being driven for over four months, Craig's grey Subaru Forester purred into life. She placed a hand on Craig's knee and asked him, "Are you all right?"

He nodded, but she could see the pain in his eyes from struggling to get into the car. She turned to Samwell in the back and said, "Sawa."

"Sawa, Memsaab," he replied.

The journey to the animal orphanage was only fifteen minutes, and the road was smooth and tarmacked as far as the Mount Kenya Resort and Spa. They turned away from the hotel entrance and bounced uncomfortably along a rutted track for two hundred metres, before turning towards the entrance of the animal orphanage. Rose parked in a shaded area under an open-fronted wooden shed.

Julius turned to close the entrance gate and then strode to meet them. He rushed forward to help

Samwell manoeuvre Craig from the car into the wheelchair, and then stood back proclaiming, "Bwana Hardie, today is truly fine as you are visiting with Mama Rose. Welcome."

He rushed back to reopen the entrance gate and ushered his guests through. Rose carried her green medical bag, but he insisted on taking it from her as he led them towards a small, single-storey stone building, in the centre of a lawned area.

"The baby ostriches are inside." He looked uncertainly from Rose to Craig.

In a bright voice Craig said, "Don't worry about me. I'd like to see the mountain bongo." He turned and looked up at Samwell, who was pushing his wheelchair. "Have you ever seen bongo?"

Samwell narrowed his eyes in confusion and shook his head.

"Then you're in for a treat." As Samwell pushed Craig's wheelchair towards the bongo paddock, Rose heard Craig lecturing him about the Mount Kenya Wildlife Conservancy's programme to replenish the number of bongo,

Africa's rarest antelope, in its original Mount Kenya habitat.

She followed Julius into his office and opened a brown cardboard box. Inside, she discovered two fawn-coloured birds with long necks, wide eyes and unstable legs. Their backs were covered in fluffy down rather than the beautiful feathers they would develop as adults.

They immediately started moving around the box, pecking curiously and attempting to escape their confined space. Rose knew that small, vulnerable baby ostriches made an enticing meal in the wild, so they developed the ability to run, almost as soon as they emerged from their shells.

As she gazed at the small figures, she hoped they would survive and grow to their full size, as the largest bird species in the world.

She turned, looked up at Julius, and asked, "Where do you propose keeping them? They're too large for the brooder boxes you have here, but they will need a heated, draught-free environment."

Julius nodded and responded, "I've asked two of my men to line one of the indoor animal enclosures with cardboard from discarded boxes, to provide extra insulation and to stop cold air seeping in. We are proposing to hang a heat lamp from the ceiling, but suspend it high enough that the ostriches cannot reach it. Do you think we should cover the floor with sawdust?"

"Yes, at least to start with. But these inquisitive birds may soon peck the cardboard to bits." She looked back at the ostriches and said, "And as we don't know where they've come from, I propose we begin by washing them with an iodine solution to guard against bacterial infection."

Rose stood up and reached for her bag as Julius asked, "What shall we feed them?"

She searched her bag and removed a bottle of dark purple-coloured liquid which she placed on Julius's desk.

She leaned against the edge and said, "Ordinarily, I wouldn't offer food or water until the chicks are about a week old, as they have fluid in their feathers that needs to be absorbed. But as we don't know what these two have been through, I recommend placing a shallow dish of water in their pen. They may not know how to drink, so see if you can find a brightly coloured dish, and a small mirror which you can place at the bottom of it, and hopefully that will attract them to the water bowl. It's important to keep them hydrated."

She turned and looked at the young ostriches. "As for food, I suggest some finely chopped alfalfa. Do you have any?"

Julius shook his head and raised his hands.

She leaned towards him. "Don't worry, I have some growing in my shamba. It's a key ingredient for my herbal mixes. I'll pick some when I get home and send it up here with a boda boda. It would also aid their digestion to add very small pieces of grit to their food, about the size of grains of rice."

Julius placed a hand on his chest and said soberly, "Thank you, Mama Rose. I really appreciate your help."

Rose pushed herself away from the table, turned and picked up the iodine bottle. "Let's get these little ones washed and inspect their new enclosure," she announced.

Julius carried the box of ostriches to a secure external pen, which extended out from the internal enclosure where they were to be housed. Rose diluted the iodine in a bucket of water. Julius put on a pair of leather gloves and picked up the first small ostrich, which twisted its long neck and pecked at him.

"Keep it steady," said Rose, as she carefully wiped its body with the solution. After completing the process with both birds, they introduced them to their new enclosure. One moved forward, wobbled on its long legs, and then scurried towards the far wall. After a moment's hesitation, the second one followed.

Rose watched the birds explore their new environment. One even ventured over to the water tray but did not drink from it.

"The temperature in here needs to be kept at around thirty degrees centigrade for the next few days, and then it can be dropped to between twenty-six and twenty-nine degrees," she said. "I'll send the alfalfa for them to eat and we'll see how they get on."

CHAPTER THREE

Rose and Julius left a member of the orphanage staff to watch over the young ostriches.

"I'd like your advice, Mama Rose, on the rehabilitation of the four orphaned jackals we've been caring for," said Julius. "They're at least eight months old now and are ready to be reintroduced into the wild."

Rose and Julius left the central orphanage area, which housed the smaller animals and the monkeys, and moved into an area that was divided into paddocks for those animals that needed room to move around, such as the pair of resident leopards. Rose spotted Samwell ahead of them and they joined him and Craig at the jackal pen.

"Everything all right?" asked Craig.

Rose stood next to him and placed a hand on his shoulder. "Yes, the ostriches are very sweet, and they're scuttling around exploring their new home."

She spotted two jackals curled up under the shade of a small, rough-leafed shepherd tree.

Craig enquired, "Julius, what's the story with these jackals?"

Julius leaned against the post and rail fence and watched the slumbering animals. "They've been with us for over seven months. There are four of them, one male and three females, and they are all black-backed jackals, which we believe are from the same litter.

"They were found abandoned next to their den, on the edge of Borana Conservancy, close to a village. Although nobody admitted it, we suspect someone in the village killed their mother, thinking she was praying on livestock."

Craig tapped his thigh. "But I thought they only scavenged in villages, or chased after rats and mice."

Julius turned but continued leaning against the fence. "That is correct, Bwana Hardie, but unfortunately some of these villagers are ignorant and blame animals for stealing their sheep when it is more likely to be a neighbour."

He sniffed. "Two askaris from Borana watched the pups and den overnight hoping their mother would return. But when she didn't, the manager asked if we could rear them until they were ready to be reintegrated into the wild."

He stepped towards Rose. "That time has come, Mama. How do you suggest we release them safely into the conservancy?"

Rose rubbed her hands together whilst she thought. "You and your team have done a sterling job raising them. But it won't be easy releasing them back into the wild, as jackals are very territorial. Have you spoken to the management team at Borana about a suitable location?"

Julius nodded. "They've been watching an empty den near the newly constructed Aureus Lodge. They think the building work scared away the pair who occupied it and they haven't returned. I would like to see it, but I don't have the transport."

Craig tapped Rose's leg. "Isn't that where Marina is working? Perhaps she can organise a vehicle for Julius."

Rose looked down at him and responded, "Or if Thabiti is visiting the lodge, he could take him."

Julius clapped his hands together. "Thank you for your suggestions, Bwana. Mama Rose, will you accompany me?"

She looked at Craig and hesitated.

"Of course, she will," Craig declared and he smiled widely.

Rose was delighted that Craig was so positive and enthusiastic. It appeared that their outing to the orphanage had been a success.

Julius and Samwell assisted Craig into the car. Rose drove back to Nanyuki through a small, nameless village, which had sprung up around a bend in the road. She spotted a figure clothed in black, with a bouncing ponytail of blonde hair, emerge from a track in front of them.

"Is that Chloe?" asked Craig. "Does she just like running or is she training for the Lewa Marathon?"

"Oh, I think she's doing the marathon. Let's ask her."

Rose slowed down as they drove alongside Chloe, who looked across and did a double take. She reduced her pace to a walk and waited for them, with her hands on her hips and her chest heaving as she caught her breath.

Rose leant over Craig and wound down the window. "Have you been running up the mountain?" she called.

"Hi, I didn't recognise the car. Yes, Thabiti and I found some tracks a couple of weeks ago, which I've been exploring. It's given me a great hill workout." She peered into the vehicle. "Where have you all been?"

"To the animal orphanage," Craig explained. "Rose has a couple of new patients."

Chloe bit her lip and looked at the ground.

Rose waited.

"Can we meet up for a chat later? At our usual place. Say half eleven?" Chloe looked at Rose and then quickly averted her eyes to stare down the road.

Rose had noted dark circles under Chloe's eyes and her pleading expression. "Of course," she replied, "As long as I'm back by lunch. Is that OK with you?" She rested a hand on Craig's thigh.

"Don't worry about me. I think I'll have a rest after this morning's outing," Craig responded.

They watched Chloe's lithe athletic figure cross the road and bound down a track towards Nanyuki.

CHAPTER FOUR

The usual place where Rose met Chloe was a corner table in Dormans coffee shop's outdoor courtyard, in the centre of Nanyuki. Rose still thought of the cafe as Dormans, despite it changing its name to 'I Love Nanyuki Coffee Shop', with a new logo resembling a t-shirt she'd once seen with 'I Love NY' on it.

She was relieved to find a parking space in front of the building which housed the cafe, upmarket gift shop and various other businesses, including a travel agent and internet company. She was greeted by the bearded face of Jack, the DVD seller. He held up a fan shape of cellophane-wrapped, pirated DVD copies of newly released films.

"Something to watch today, Mama?" he suggested, waving his goods.

"No, thank you," Rose responded curtly, but then she regretted being so rude. Whilst she didn't agree with the practice of selling illegal copies of DVDs, she recognised that Jack was just trying to make a living and only pirate copies were available in Nanyuki. "OK, let me see what you have," she conceded.

He arranged the DVDs like a pack of cards and showed her the top one, which depicted a man with a large gun. She shook her head. He shuffled the DVDs, revealing several more images of men with guns or cars.

"What's that about?" she asked.

He held up a film with a dog on the cover. "It's about a small robot dog which can talk to the military and helps them save people."

She looked up at Jack and shook her head. "Sorry, it's not really my thing."

He picked up a plastic bag, which contained more of his stock, and wandered away to join other street sellers who were loitering by the wall, at the end of the Dormans complex.

She strode through a metal-framed arch and was greeted by a smiling Marina sitting at a long wooden table facing the entrance.

Marina placed her hands on the table and propelled herself to a standing position. "Mama Rose, I've got some exciting news for you!" cried Marina.

Rose glanced over to the corner table, but it was empty. Chloe had not arrived yet.

A young waiter stepped forward and pulled the heavy wooden bench out so she could sit opposite Marina. "What would you like to drink?" he asked.

Rose smiled up at him. "Thank you. Can I have a Kericho Gold tea, please?"

"Anything to eat?"

She shook her head. "No, thanks."

Marina grabbed Rose's arm. "So you know we were expecting the family to arrive soon, the ones who own the lodge? Well, the wife has damaged her Achilles tendon and can't run in the Lewa Marathon, so they've postponed their visit."

Rose pursed her lips. "But isn't that rather disappointing? I thought they might offer you a full-time position if they liked you."

Marina raised her hands and shrugged. "Don't get me wrong, it's a great opportunity and the lodge is amazing, but do you know what? I don't think I want to spend the rest of my life constantly repeating orders to staff members and tending to the wants and wishes of wealthy people."

She leaned forward and dropped her voice. "I spoke to Lavi, who's preparing to leave for her mission in northern Kenya, and she's really excited at the thought of helping people. I need to feel that sort of passion, and it's not going to come from checking that shampoo bottles have been refilled to the correct level in the ensuite bathrooms."

Marina sat back and drummed the table. "But that's not why I'm excited. Although some friends of the owners are coming instead, Ollie says you and Craig can stay as well. In fact, he said having more people will be a good way of testing and training the staff. What do you think?" Her eyes shone.

"Well, I'm not sure. I'll need to discuss it with Craig. And I'm not sure if Chris is staying with us."

"Chris?" Marina drew her eyebrows together and sat up. "Who's Chris?"

"My son." Rose pulled a vase of red and yellow roses towards her. She sniffed, but whilst they were colourful, and brightened up the courtyard, they had no fragrance. She pushed the vase back to the centre of the table and looked at Marina.

"Didn't you meet him at the Mount Kenya Resort and Spa before the Giant's Club Summit in April?"

Marina shook her head vigorously. "No, I left with a tour group for Samburu, the day after the Laikipia Conservation Society conference."

Rose leaned back. "Of course you did. Well, I've barely seen Chris since he left school and joined the British Army over fifteen years ago, but he was working as part of a security team at the summit."

She waited whilst the waiter placed a white cup, with the cafe logo printed on its side, on the table in front of her. He also set down a foil-wrapped teabag and two white jugs containing hot water and milk.

Rose continued, "We caught up briefly, but I've been asking him to return to Kenya to see us, particularly as Craig is ill. And he emailed to say he's running in the Lewa Marathon next weekend."

Marina slapped the table. "That's fantastic news. You must be really excited about seeing him again."

Rose tore open the foil packet and extracted the teabag. As she made her tea, she reflected that she wasn't exactly excited, rather she felt a mixture of hope and anxiety.

It was important to her that Craig and Chris settled their differences and spent some quality time together. She hoped Chris would stay with them, at least some of the time, rather than with his army mates.

"He's arriving on Saturday, but I'm not sure what his plans are." She stirred milk into her cup.

Marina shrugged. "Why not invite him as well? The more the merrier."

Rose smiled thankfully at Marina. "I'll let Chris know about your kind offer. And I'll speak with Craig, but I think he would like to come. His trip to the animal orphanage today really cheered him up." She scratched her neck. "But he's now using a wheelchair. Is that a problem?"

Marina playfully tapped Rose's arm. "Not at all. It's fabulous that he's able to get around. And it'll be good practice for our staff."

Marina leaned forward conspiratorially. "I need your help with something." She looked around and continued. "As the family aren't coming, they offered me their places in the marathon."

She sat up and raised her arms to shoulder height. "Of course I'm not marathon fit. And I won't be able to run the entire way like Chloe. But loads of people just walk round so they can then say they've completed the 'Lewa

Marathon'. I thought Thabiti and I could do it together, but he's reluctant. I think he's worried by all the people who'll be there, and that they'll be judging him for being unfit and only walking round."

Rose raised her eyebrows, "So you want me to persuade him to take part?"

"Exactly," cried Marina. "I know he listens to you."

"It's not really my place, but I'll see what I can do." Rose lifted her teacup.

CHAPTER FIVE

Rose was sitting with her back to the entrance of Dormans' courtyard so she couldn't see who entered. A voice greeted her, "Hi, Rose. It's a while since I've seen you here."

She turned and looked up at the round, intelligent face of Stella McDonald. "Hello, Stella, it's lovely to see you. I've actually been spending more time with Craig recently. Besides, I thought you were away on one of your work trips."

Stella fiddled with her glasses and replied, "Yes, I was. I returned yesterday from a two-week trip to Honduras, which has the unenviable record of being the murder capital of the world. Still, despite twenty deaths a day, we're supporting communities which are slowly taking back their neighbourhoods from the gangs, so there is hope for a brighter future."

"Wow, that sounds fascinating," exclaimed Marina.

"It is. Hi, I'm Stella." She reached over and offered her hand to Marina, who shook it vigorously.

Marina admitted, "I'd love to be involved in work like that. It must be so satisfying."

Stella leaned towards Marina, examining her and said, "Well, we are looking for volunteers. Some younger people like you who don't mind roughing it, and who are willing to work at our remote 'aid project' bases."

Rose pushed back the heavy wooden bench, which scraped unwillingly across the tiled floor. She stood up and announced, "I think you two should discuss this further." She turned to Stella. "For what it's worth, I think Marina would be a fantastic addition to your team."

She looked across at Marina who beamed.

"Sorry I'm late," called Chloe as she reached Rose's side. "Hi, Marina."

"How's the training going?" asked Marina.

Stella sat down on the bench Rose had vacated.

Chloe bounced on her toes. "Not bad. I ran a route up the mountain today which Thabiti and I discovered."

Rose took Chloe's arm. "I've been having a good chat with Marina, but look, our table's still empty. Shall we sit down?"

Rose and Chloe walked away, leaving Stella and Marina in animated discussion.

"How's Marina getting on at the lodge?" Chloe asked as she sat on one of four wooden seats attached to a picnic style table in the corner of Dormans' courtyard. Behind her, the usually dusty green-leafed plants were clean and gleamed in the sunlight.

The young waiter carried Rose's teacup and saucer across, placing them on the table in front of her.

She had forgotten about her tea. "Thank you," she said to the waiter.

Chloe picked up the menu and commented to Rose. "I should have the Healthy Juice option, but I feel like I need a cappuccino."

She looked up at the patient waiter and asked, "Can I have the breakfast avocado salad with two poached eggs and a cappuccino?" She tapped the menu on the table and looked at Rose. "You don't mind me eating, do you? I need something after that run as my stomach's aching and I feel a little light-headed."

The waiter retreated inside the coffee shop.

Chloe drummed her fingers. "So, Marina. She looks happy."

"I think everything's going well at the lodge, although the family isn't coming next week as planned. Apparently, the wife is injured and can't run in the marathon, so some friends are staying instead. Marina has invited Craig and me to stay over the marathon weekend, too, and Chris if he wants to come."

Chloe leaned towards Rose. "I didn't know he was visiting. That's fantastic news. When does he arrive?"

Rose lifted her teacup. "Saturday. After arriving from the UK, he's flying up from Nairobi, instead of driving."

Chloe leaned back and rubbed her chin. "But you don't look particularly excited."

Rose sighed. "This is probably the last time he's going to see Craig. I've been praying for him to come back and visit, but what if they don't settle their differences, or worse still, fall out again?"

Chloe clutched her hands together. "I'm sure Chris knows how important it is to make things right with his father, for your sake at the very least. They are both grown-ups, so they need to sort out their own issues. Although that's often easier said than done." Chloe looked down and twisted her gold wedding band.

Rose realised they had come to the reason Chloe had requested their meeting. She leaned forward and placed her hand on Chloe's arm. "What's happened? Is it something to do with Dan?"

Chloe sniffed and wiped an eye with the back of her hand. "I don't know what to do," she sobbed. "I thought things were better after the

Rhino Charge. I took your advice, and asked him how he felt and what he wanted to do. But now we end up spending most of the time when he's home with the British Army guys.

"I had enough of that back in the UK and I thought the point of moving here was for a fresh start. And that we would meet new people, not a variation of the ones we used to meet up with, who can only talk about their work and the failings of the army system."

Chloe picked up Rose's teaspoon and tapped it against her arm. Watching it, she continued, "And they complain constantly about living in Kenya and that their military TV channels don't show the football matches they want to see."

She looked up at Rose. "Why don't they just visit a bar in town? I'm always seeing signs advertising football match screenings. And to cap it all, Dan has clammed up and won't speak to me about anything meaningful."

When the young waiter arrived with Chloe's order, she bowed her head and rubbed her forehead to hide her face.

"Thank you," Rose said to the waiter.

"Do you need any sauces?" he enquired.

Chloe briefly shook her head.

"No, we're fine, thank you," Rose answered.

Chloe lifted her head and smoothed down her long blond hair. Whilst she unwrapped the cutlery from her napkin, and picked up her knife and fork, Rose had a chance to examine her more closely.

In her mid-to-late thirties, Chloe had arrived in Nanyuki only four months previously, and she'd cut an elegant figure in her designer clothes and impractical high-heeled shoes.

Although her face was now tanned, Rose noticed small horizontal lines at the corners of her eyes and several across her forehead.

She thought that the work pattern for Chloe's husband Dan, which involved a lot of time away on his own at a large construction camp in the north of Kenya, was beginning to damage their marriage.

Especially as Chloe was also worried about not being able to have children, and the frequent miscarriages she had admitted having.

Rose allowed Chloe time to compose herself. She watched her break the yoke of a poached egg so that it ran across the top of the green avocado and lettuce mix, until it reached the small red halves of cherry tomatoes at the edge of the bowl.

"When is Dan home next?" Rose asked gently.

Chloe finished chewing and answered, "Wednesday. We're running the Lewa Marathon together on Saturday."

"Well, maybe that's your opportunity to reconnect. Completing the marathon is a real feat."

"We're only running the half-marathon."

"Oh, don't worry about that. Only elite athletes and the completely insane run the full marathon. It's not twice as hard as the half, more like ten times, especially as the temperature rises dramatically during the morning."

Chloe bowed her head and ate another mouthful of breakfast.

Rose said, "I know you don't want to natter at him, but it might be worth suggesting a few nights away at a lodge after the marathon, as long as he's not returning straight back to work.

"It could give you a chance to talk things through. I find the open savannah clears my head and gives me a better perspective on my life and problems."

Chloe put down her knife and fork and dabbed her eyes with her napkin. She smiled weakly at Rose. "I'll do that. Where do you suggest?"

CHAPTER SIX

Rose returned home expecting to find Craig resting quietly, but she heard laughter as she walked around the side of her cottage.

"That's a ridiculous answer," called Craig. He was sitting on his large cedar chair, with its striped kikoi cushions, whilst Thabiti was sitting at the dining table, twirling a pencil in his hand. A piece of paper lay in front of him, which Rose presumed was a crossword puzzle.

"It's not a complicated clue," chided Craig. "It just needs some knowledge of modern history. The answer is the name of the warring country which was reunited in 1975."

Thabiti threw up his arms. "I wasn't alive in 1975, so how would I know the answer? And I don't consider that modern history."

Craig tutted. "I don't know what they taught you at school. The answer is Vietnam."

Thabiti started to write the answer on the piece of paper but asked, "How do you spell that?"

Rose saw Craig pinch his lips together so she stepped across and stood beside Thabiti. She peered at the puzzle but shook her head. "I can't read it without my glasses."

Thabiti wrote 'VIETNAM' in large letters at the top of the piece of paper.

"Yes, I think that's right, and that's enough sparring between you two for today."

"I'm only teasing him," said Craig.

She moved to his side and placed a hand on his shoulder. "I know, and whilst thinking and having some banter is good, you still have to be careful. I know your blood pressure is rising by the colour of your face."

Papers were scattered across the cushions on the large wooden sofa. She gathered them up and noticed tables of numbers and photographs of cultivated crops.

"I saw Marina in Dormans," she reported as she sat down. "Apparently the family who own the lodge aren't coming next week after all."

Thabiti swivelled on his dining chair, faced her and said, "I know, she phoned me earlier and told me the wife's injured herself, but they offered the main house to some friends instead."

"Did she also tell you Ollie has agreed that Craig and I can stay as well?" She turned to her husband. "That is, if you want to go."

"Oh yes, do come." Pink spots appeared on Thabiti's cheeks and he glanced down. "I'd love to show you around Waitabit Farm in person, where Borana conservancy is slow growing its own fruit and vegetables. And we could discuss the potential for some form of hydroponic agriculture at the lodge."

Craig rubbed his chin, "But what about Chris? Do we know if he's planning to stay with us?"

She shrugged. "I haven't heard anything more from him. Marina thinks it would be fine for him to stay as well, although I suspect he'll want to be with his army teammates over the marathon weekend. We could see if he wants to join us for a night or two before or after."

"And talking of the marathon." Rose turned to Thabiti, who shrank back. "I understand the family has offered Marina and you their entries. She thinks it's a great opportunity, and I agree. Do you know that places in the marathon are expensive and hard to come by?"

Thabiti stuffed his hands in his pockets.

Rose continued. "She said that she's not as fit as Chloe, and couldn't run the whole way, but perhaps the two of you could walk round. Lots of people do that. I know some of the army wives and Podo School mums have been in training to jog and walk the event this year."

Thabiti crossed his legs. "Wives and mums. I bet the husbands and dads aren't walking. They'll be running with the British army and I'll look like an idiot shuffling along at the back with all those women."

"I wouldn't be too worried," said Craig. "Everyone will be too anxious about their own performance to be interested in you. I presume this is for the half marathon?"

"Yes," nodded Rose.

Craig placed his hands on the arms of his chair to support himself as he leaned closer to Thabiti. "In my experience, it's impossible to tell who's doing the half and who's running the full marathon, and people run and walk at different stages during the race. You're pretty fit, so you could combine running and walking. Have you ever been to the Lewa Marathon?"

"No," admitted Thabiti, uncrossing his legs and scraping his feet across the tiled floor.

"It really is a spectacle, with long lines of competitors snaking their way along tracks across the vast Lewa Downs. I've never competed, but I love the atmosphere of hope, determination and, to an extent, suffering as runners battle their own internal demons, as well as the external demands of one of the toughest marathon courses in the world. I think it's a fantastic opportunity and not one you're likely to be offered again anytime soon."

Rose clasped her hands together. "And you're young and fit. And Marina is very excited. Surely you don't want to let her down. If you're worried about what people will say or think, hide under a baseball cap or something."

Thabiti removed his hands from his pockets and clasped them together. "I'll think about it," he said grudgingly.

Rose raised her hand to her lips, thinking. "There was something else I needed to ask you."

Craig peered at her over his glasses. "Was it about Julius and the jackals?"

"Ah yes," she smiled at him and turned back to Thabiti. "Julius and his team at the Animal Orphanage have been raising four orphaned jackals, which were found on Borana at the end of last year. They're ready to be released back into the conservancy and he's been told about an empty den near Aureus Lodge.

"He's looking for a lift over there to check it out, and he's asked me to go with him. I wondered if you were planning a day visit early next week and could give us both a lift?"

Thabiti pulled his legs together and said, "Marina's asked me to go on Tuesday and deliver some furniture she's ordered. It might be a bit of a squash on the way there."

Craig tapped his leg. "I'm sure Julius can put up with that."

Rose sat up and looked at Thabiti. "So we'll plan for a day visit on Tuesday with Julius." She turned to Craig. "And shall we go to the lodge on Thursday and stay for the weekend?"

Craig nodded. "Why not? As long as Marina and her team are happy to help me. Then I can give Samwell a few days off. Will Thursday be OK, Thabiti?"

Thabiti shrugged. "I guess so. I think I'm heading back on Wednesday with more furniture and whatever supplies Marina needs, and then I'll stay down for a while as we make the lodge fully operational. The owner's friends and the yoga group are due to arrive on Thursday, too."

CHAPTER SEVEN

Nanyuki airstrip was located ten kilometres south of the town centre. It was small with a single runway which received guests on commercial flights from Nairobi, then distributed them in smaller planes to lodges around Laikipia and beyond.

Some guests stayed near Nanyuki, either at the Mount Kenya Resort and Spa or on Ol Pejeta Conservancy. The airport was also home to Equator Air, an aviation company with small and medium-sized planes and five helicopters.

Rose parked Craig's Subaru by a duranta hedge which separated the runway from the rest of the small airport. A pair of tall black metal gates provided access to the airstrip.

Despite it being Saturday, a group of excited, teenage African schoolchildren gathered by the hedge. Dressed in their yellow uniforms, they grabbed hold of each other and pointed at a blue helicopter as its large blades began to turn.

Rose extracted herself from the car and watched as the blades spun in a whirl and the helicopter lifted itself up into the clear blue sky, banked right and flew away to the north. The children cried out and waved it on its journey.

She looked around to see if there was anyone who could help her move Craig from the car into his wheelchair.

Jono Urquhart, one of the pilots with Equator Air, was peering inside an open panel on the side of a blue caravan: a medium-sized aeroplane which could carry up to twelve passengers. He looked across and she beckoned to him.

As he opened the black metal gate he said, "Morning, Rose, is everything OK?"

"Jono, it's good to see you. I wondered if you could help my husband into his wheelchair." She opened the boot of the Subaru and Jono reached in and pulled out the folded wheelchair.

"Of course," he said as he opened the chair, made sure it was secure and wheeled it forward.

Craig opened the passenger door. "Thank you. It's irritating having to rely on other people, but I've decided it's better than staying at home."

Rose held the wheelchair steady and Jono half-lifted and half-dragged Craig across into it.

Jono stood up smiling and said, "I hope I wasn't too rough."

Craig's face was pinched with pain, but he answered, "Not at all. I appreciate the help."

Rose squatted down and arranged Craig's feet comfortably on the footrest.

"I'm flying a group over to Baringo shortly, so I won't be here to help you back into the car," Jono explained. He turned towards a small, single-storey wooden building between the hedge and airstrip and raised a hand in its direction. "But if you ask at the office they should be able to find someone to assist you."

Rose stood. "Thank you. We're meeting our son from the SAX flight from Nairobi, so he'll be able to help." She touched Jono's arm and asked quietly, "How are you? Have you seen Lavi recently?"

Jono swallowed. "I'm flying down to Nairobi this afternoon and spending the weekend with her. It will be our last together, as she's catching the bus to Lodwar next week. I don't know when I'll see her after that, or even if I'll be allowed to." He looked away, up the airstrip in the direction the helicopter had flown.

Rose gently squeezed his arm.

She pushed Craig and his wheelchair through a gap in another hedge, which ran at right angles to the airstrip and enclosed Barney's restaurant. This was a favourite spot to grab a drink or a meal before or after a flight.

It also provided a welcome change from the restaurants in Nanyuki, and families often visited as their children could entertain themselves on the wooden swings, or climb on the back of the decorative metal rhino and watch the planes and helicopters land and take-off on the airstrip.

There was a covered raised platform with tables and chairs, a small gift shop and access to the restaurant kitchen. Rose was relieved to find an empty table at ground level, next to the platform. A waiter rushed over and pulled a chair away from the table.

"Let me help." He reversed the wheelchair and then parked it in the empty space.

 Rose peered at his name tag which she thought said Geoffrey. She looked up and recognised the waiter from Barney's sister restaurant, the Bushman in Nanyuki.

"Thank you. I thought your name was Geoff."

The waiter grinned at her. "That's my twin."

He left them and Rose pondered, "I presume he was joking, and that he works here and at the Bushman, but has different name badges."

Craig chortled. "I don't think anyone would call one twin Geoff and the other Geoffrey, but you never know."

Geoffrey returned with heavy, red, leatherbound menus as they heard the low hum of an approaching plane.

Craig checked his watch. "This should be Chris's flight."

A small commercial red and white plane flew low over them, turned and approached the airstrip from the north. Fascinated, they watched its progress as its wheels bounced once, then twice, on the concrete runway before they heard a rushing-air noise as the thrust reversers were deployed and the plane slowed.

It was out of sight for a couple of minutes, but they could hear a loud whirring noise and then it reappeared, slowly taxiing towards them with the front propeller still spinning. The plane parked ten metres away from the black metal gates and as the blade speed reduced, so did the noise.

They couldn't see the passengers disembark, but shortly after landing, a smartly dressed African man walked towards the now open metal gate. He carried a briefcase and strode across to a black Toyota Land Cruiser parked three cars away from Craig's Subaru.

Next to appear was a couple who looked as if they had stepped out of one of the upmarket magazines that Rose occasionally flicked through at Cape Chestnut restaurant.

They both wore light brown cargo-style trousers, neutral coloured cotton shirts, and multi-pocketed khaki-coloured waistcoats. The man stood tall, wearing a fawn, Australian stockman style, Akubra hat, and stared around as if expecting someone to meet them. His posture became rigid and Rose had the impression he was annoyed to be left standing on the tarmac.

Behind them Chris emerged, dressed in shorts and a polo shirt with the strap of his black canvas bag looped over his shoulder.

Rose stood and waved.

Chris smiled in recognition and walked past the couple, through the open metal gate and around the hedge into Barney's. "Hi Mum." He dropped his bag to the floor and tentatively placed his arms around her thin frame, gently hugging her. He looked into her face. "You look well."

Rose stood back, amazed by how fine and handsome her son was, although he needed some colour in his pasty white face. "It's great to see you."

Chris stepped behind her and faced his father across the table. "Dad," he said, in a matter-of-fact tone, and extended his arm.

Craig took the proffered hand, clasped it in both of his and declared, "It's good to have you home."

CHAPTER EIGHT

C hris and Rose sat side by side, opposite Craig.

Chris clasped his hands on the table in front of him. "Thanks for coming to meet me." He picked up a menu. "Since we're here, why don't we have an early lunch? My flight was late in last night and by the time I reached the hotel I didn't feel like supper. I grabbed a coffee at Wilson Airport this morning, but I need something more substantial."

Rose and Craig looked at each other.

"My treat," said Chris, as he opened one of the menus. He exclaimed, "Feta and coriander samosas. I haven't had those in years." He looked at his parents with a boyish grin between his chubby cheeks. "Shall we share a portion to start with?" His sharp blue eyes shone with delight and mischief.

Just then, the man with the Akubra hat bumped Chris's shoulder with his bag. "Oh, I'm terribly sorry." He stopped, stepped back and asked, "Weren't you on our flight from Nairobi? Are you a local?" he asked with an edge of derision in his voice.

Chris leaned back in the green canvas safari chair and crossed his arms over his chest. "Sorry. No. I've just arrived from London. And I'm here visiting my parents." He nodded towards Rose and Craig.

"Oh, well, perhaps you could help us?" The man turned towards Craig. "My wife and I are staying at the Lake Lodge in Ol Pejeta Conservancy. And we were told a car would pick us up, but nobody is here to meet us." He wrinkled his nose.

Craig looked at the man over his spectacles and reassured him, "Don't worry. I've heard they're repairing parts of the road out to Ol Pejeta at the moment and there are some lengthy detours. I'm sure your vehicle is just delayed. Why don't you sit down and have a drink, or something to eat, whilst you wait?"

The man sighed in relief. "Thank you. That's a jolly good suggestion. I was half afraid we'd been told to get off at the wrong rustic airstrip. Come on, darling," he drawled to his female companion, and climbed the steps onto the platform without offering to help carry her bag.

Craig shook his head and commented, "And people wonder why we lost the empire and the Kenyan's wanted their country back."

Rose watched the man fold himself into a safari chair and lift up a menu whilst his wife or girlfriend, she was not sure which, dropped her bag on the floor, rolled her shoulders back and gingerly sat down.

Craig turned to Chris and asked, "So what are your plans whilst you're here?"

Chris leant forward, resting his arms on the table, and replied, "If it's OK with you, I'll hang around at yours for a few days, have a bit of a rest and see who else is around. I'm staying in BATUK's tented camp on Lewa on Friday before the marathon, and I expect there'll be a party afterwards. Apart from that, I'm pretty flexible." He smiled broadly.

A small plane with 'Safari Link' painted on the side touched down on the runway.

Rose leaned forward. "Of course you can stay with us. And you can have one of the guest cottages, so you've got some space to yourself."

The Safari Link plane slowed to a stop by the metal gate.

She looked down at the table and said, "And we've been asked to stay at a brand-new lodge on Borana over the marathon weekend. I'm sure you'd be welcome as well."

The muscles in Chris's face tensed.

She added quickly. "But you don't have to decide now."

In the silence that followed, Rose watched an elegantly dressed woman emerge from the plane. She wore a floppy wide-brimmed hat with a bright red bow and tailored red shorts, and carried a smart leather weekend bag.

Chris still smiled, but it was now a thin line. "Shall we look at the menu?" he suggested.

Craig coughed to clear his throat. "I believe there's a specials board as well by the kitchen. Or we could ask Geoffrey." He caught the waiter's eyes and beckoned to him.

The elegant lady strode purposefully through the entrance to Barney's and up onto the platform. She stopped and exclaimed, "Robert, by all that's wonderful, what are you doing here?"

The man, Robert, pushed back his chair, stood and said hesitantly, "Why, Vivian, what an unexpected pleasure. My wife and I are on honeymoon. I don't think you've met Nina." He indicated towards his female companion with an outstretched arm.

Rose realised how young Nina was, probably barely into her twenties. She gave Rose the impression of a frightened baby antelope taking its first tentative steps on unsteady legs, whilst being aware that a predator's eyes were watching her.

"It's lovely to meet you," enthused Vivian. "Is this your first time in Keenya?" She announced the last word in the colonial manner with a long 'e' sound. "Oh, what a lovely ring!" She grasped Nina's hand and examined her gold rings, which glinted in the sunlight.

"Mum," Chris interrupted Rose's musings. "Are you interested in any of the specials Geoffrey has just told us?"

She turned back and found three expectant faces watching her. "I'd like the quiche and salad, please." She smiled apologetically at Geoffrey. "And as we're celebrating the arrival of my son, a glass of wine. And can I also have a small bottle of sparkling water?" Why not have a glass of wine? She was celebrating and Chris had offered to pay.

As Geoffrey departed, she heard the elegant woman on the decking above announce, "But you must have a hat if you're going on safari. Especially with your fair complexion. Here, try on mine."

Rose watched Nina shrink back. But it wasn't far enough, as Vivian whipped off her hat, revealing shoulder length glossy brunette hair, and planted her hat over Nina's mousy blonde bob. Nina disappeared under the large floppy hat.

"Perfect," announced Vivian. "Where are you heading?"

Robert replied, "Ol Pejeta. We're staying at Lake Lodge."

"Oh lovely," Vivian exclaimed. "I've just been staying on Lewa."

Rose heard the blast of a car horn.

Vivian swung round. "Ah, there's my lift." She bent down and pecked Robert on both cheeks. "Catch you later, darling." She skipped down the steps towards a long wheelbase safari vehicle, with its canvas sides rolled up.

Rose turned back as Geoffrey placed their drinks on the table. "So how is London?" she asked her son.

"You know, it's a great place to be based. Increasingly my work takes me abroad and Heathrow has excellent air links. And then, when I'm at home, everything's so convenient. London really spruced itself up for the 2012 Olympics, and there's a real sense of pride. As I was leaving, the weather was warming up and cafes and restaurants were beginning to set up their outdoor tables and chairs. That brings an Italian feel to the city in summer."

Craig cleared his throat again. "And is there anyone special in your life?" he asked.

Rose waited. This was a question she'd longed to ask but hadn't been able to pluck up the courage to do so.

Chris closed his eyes and pinched the bridge of his nose. "There was for a while, after I left the army. A girl called Amy, but she had a young daughter who became increasingly unsettled as my trips away with work increased. We split up, but I guess it's for the best. Besides, I'm not sure I really want the ties of a relationship. I like being free to choose when and where I go."

CHAPTER NINE

Out of the corner of her eye, Rose saw Chris lean against the uneven post-and-rail fence, which enclosed her grass paddock.

"Sit up," she shouted at the ten-year-old African boy who was tilted forward over the neck of the grey pony he rode.

He slapped his legs against the pony's side and flapped his elbows.

"It's a pony, not a wind up car. Kicking madly and waving your arms about won't make him go any faster. Now sit up and push him forward with your bottom," she instructed.

The boy sat up and began pushing his bottom into the saddle.

"OK, now you can give him a kick."

The boy hit the pony's sides with his heels, and it jumped forward into a canter.

"Good. Sit up and look forward. If he starts to slow down, push with your bottom and squeeze him forward with your legs."

The boy and his pony completed a lap of the paddock.

"Well done," called Rose. "Bring him back to a trot. Do you want to just have a ride around for a few minutes?"

Rose strolled across to Chris.

"Who's your young pupil?" he asked.

"Kipto's grandson. He's actually quite good, but like most boys, he's more interested in speed than style."

The boy trotted quickly past them with his reins slack and hanging in a loop down the pony's neck. The pony stopped abruptly by the entrance to the paddock where Kipto stood, beaming proudly. A stout African man slid a high level wooden pole out of its slot and lowered it to the ground. He stepped over and caught hold of the pony's head.

"Where did you get the pony from?" Chris asked.

"It was sent to me by the KSPCA in Nairobi. They rescued it from beside the Ngong Road where, despite its young age, it had been ridden. I'm afraid it was in a terrible state with its back rubbed raw from an ill-fitting saddle, and a hole in its withers from who knows what. We've only just been able to start riding it, but it's still very nervous."

They turned away from the paddock and walked towards the house, followed by Rose's black and tan terrier, Potto. They entered the cottage through the rear kitchen door. Kipto had returned and was tipping potatoes onto a wooden counter.

"Kongoi, Mama. Chumba loves riding the pony. He not very good with work at school but he feel much better after his ride."

"I'm so glad. And he's a good kid. What are we having for supper?"

Kipto began peeling the potatoes. "Beef stew and smash potatoes with cabbage."

Rose frowned. She presumed Kipto meant mashed potatoes, and she hoped she wouldn't boil the cabbage into submission.

Chris had already moved through into the living room and out onto the patio.

Rose followed him, but stopped in the living room as she heard him say, "Five across. Ten letters. Occurring after death. Well, that has to be 'posthumous'."

Craig answered. "That's correct." There was a pause before Craig said, "You do realise I'm dying. And it won't be long. It's as though I can feel parts of my body begin to falter."

Chris answered, "I was here when you had your mini stroke, remember, but that doesn't mean you're going to die anytime soon. People can live for years after suffering one."

"I know," responded Craig. "But it's not just the stroke. This polio thing is eating away at my body."

She and Craig had discussed his illness, and they had both accepted he would no longer be able to participate in such activities as officiating at the Rhino Charge or the Lewa Marathon. But this was the first time she had heard him talk so frankly and openly about his death.

"But it's not me I am worried about," continued Craig. "I've been very fortunate to lead a full and varied life. My crippled leg could have stopped me, but it didn't. Especially out here where people are far less judgemental and encourage one to embrace life.

"No, it's your mother I am worried about, as she'll be left alone. I do hope she'll be allowed to keep this house with its shamba, so she can grow her herbs, and the paddock and stables for her animals. But what if she has to move?"

There was a pause before Chris responded. "I've told you before, I will help her, but my life is in the UK and hers is here. She'd hate moving to London, as it would be such an alien environment to her with all the buildings, people and noise. And as I told you, I'm away a lot, so it wouldn't be very practical. If she wants to go anywhere, she would be better off with Heather."

"Your sister has her girls to look after."

"Well, I still think Mum is best here amongst her friends and people who care about her. Also, it's far cheaper to get help in Kenya than in the UK. Can you imagine if you were back there now with a full-time carer, or if you'd had to move to a nursing home? You'd hate it and the cost would be horrendous."

Craig's voice increased in pitch. "But if you're travelling around so much, why don't you come and live here? There are lots of people based in Nairobi, and even Nanyuki, who travel abroad a lot for work."

Rose heard Chris sigh. "I really don't want to fall out about this, but you do need to understand. My home is in London and I am staying there."

Rose felt torn. She understood Craig's concerns but also realised that Chris's life, and home, in the UK were important to him. The last thing she wanted was for her son and her husband to fall out over her. She stepped out onto the patio.

Chris was walking away in the direction of the guest cottage, his shoulders hunched. She knelt by Craig, who had covered his face with his hands.

"Were you listening to any of that?" he whispered.

"Yes," she replied gently.

"I only want to protect you. I can't understand why he's so stubborn," pleaded Craig. He removed his hand and looked at her with tear-filled eyes.

"He is right." She bent over and hugged him.

Back on her knees, she grasped his hands. "I have friends here and a support network. This is my home and I don't want to leave it to be cared for elsewhere, especially in England. And London is Chris's home. Please try to understand. And you two arguing only makes it harder for me. I will need his support and I won't have it if we drive him away again."

CHAPTER TEN

On Tuesday morning Rose was ready and waiting when a horn sounded outside her compound. Samwell opened the gate and closed it behind her as she climbed into the front passenger seat of Thabiti's white Land Cruiser.

Rose had rarely seen him drive it and remembered the car had belonged to his mother, a childhood friend of Rose's, who had been murdered a few months earlier.

Thabiti held a flat brown paper package and asked, "Can you nurse this? It's a painting from the UK which has just arrived and is to be hung in the dining room at the lodge."

Rose turned to the passenger in the rear and said, "Habari Julius," before taking hold of the large package and resting it on her feet.

"Mzuri sana," he replied with a large grin and pushed his hands down on the plush seat.

Their first stop was the roadside workshop of Tony the woodman, who had built his ramshackle wooden hut opposite the entrance to Podo School.

He ensured his wares of rustic tables, bookshelves, chairs, and whatever else he was currently working on, were prominently displayed by half-past eight each morning, so they would catch the eye of Podo parents leaving the school after morning drop-off.

Tony delightedly clasped each of their hands in turn. Rose realised why he was so excited when they were led around the side of his workshop and he lifted a tarpaulin to reveal a large collection of furniture.

It represented a lot of work, and an excellent income for Tony, who had only recently started his furniture business.

Thabiti consulted his phone. "Marina has asked me to take a king-size bed, two side tables and a washstand."

Tony stepped forward into the jumble melee of items, picked up a small table with a drawer and handed it to Julius. They repeated the process with another bedside table and a large table with a hole in the middle.

"That's for the sink," explained Tony. "And this is the bed." He stood proudly next to a large, solid looking piece of furniture.

Thabiti winced. "I'll never get that in my car."

Tony bent down. "We can undo these screws and take the frame apart? Would you be able to put it back together at the lodge?"

Thabiti kicked at a wood chip on the dusty ground. "I think so, as long as I don't lose the screws."

Tony whistled and an old man peered through an opening in the slats of the hut. Tony spoke rapidly to him in Kikuyu and he vanished, reappearing beside them with a screwdriver.

It took an hour to dismantle the bed and find just the right combination of pieces of furniture so that it all fitted into the car. Julius sat warily in the back, pinned between the ends of the two long sides of the bed frame which slanted up from the boot.

Thabiti was sweating and removed his fleece jumper. He turned to Julius and asked, "Are you OK back there?"

"I think so," Julius replied gingerly.

Rose picked up Thabiti's discarded jumper and said, "Why don't you wrap this around the piece of wood next to the window? It might help protect the glass, and Julius's head if we hit a bump."

"Good idea," Thabiti leant into the back and arranged the jumper over the end of the bed frame. He also shifted the leg of a table, so it didn't move during the journey and poke Julius's leg.

Thabiti drove carefully over the speed bumps as they travelled north out of Nanyuki. The first part of the drive was relatively smooth on a tarmac road. After Timau, they turned left onto a muram track and maintained a steady speed, with only a few jolts to unsettle Julius in his precarious position in the back.

Thabiti slowed at the entrance to the Ngare Ndare forest to negotiate hanging strands of thick wire.

"Why are these here?" he asked.

"To stop the elephants," shouted Julius from the back.

They continued slowly and the car rocked as Thabiti negotiated the uneven road. "I hate this bit of the drive," he said. "I'm never sure whether to try to stay on the bits of tarmac or keep completely clear of them. But at least it's dry so I can use the tracks by the side of the road without worrying that we'll slide into a tree."

"Someone told me this road was built by the British Army nearly a century ago," Rose commented, "when it was the main route north. So it's done incredibly well to survive at all."

"Well, I wish they'd repair it," quipped Thabiti, as the steering wheel jerked in his hand and Julius cried out as they slid into a large pothole.

"Sorry about that," apologised Thabiti.

Rose turned to Julius, who was rubbing his head.

"It's OK, Mama."

They drove through the main part of the forest and emerged onto a road running along the side of a cliff. There was a large drop to the right and a stunning view of the forest and, as the road turned to the left, Rose could see all the way to what she thought was the Mathews Range of hills. "Spectacular," she announced.

They arrived at Aureus Lodge and Thabiti pulled into a bare-earth parking space marked by white painted stones.

Marina ran forward to meet them and threw her arms around him.

He stood rigid with his arms by his side.

She released him and exclaimed. "It's great to see you. How was your drive?"

Before he had time to answer, Marina crossed to Rose and threw open her arms. "Welcome to Aureus Lodge."

There was a tapping sound, and they turned to see Julius peering out of the car window.

"I think he's stuck," Rose explained.

Marina called for help and between them they swiftly removed the furniture, and a shaken Julius was extracted from the car.

Marina grabbed hold of his arm and asked, "Chai?"

He nodded and was led away by a member of the lodge staff.

Rose was also enjoying a cup of refreshing tea when Julius reappeared and said, "Kennedy, the lodge gardener, is going to show us the empty den. It's about a kilometre away. Are you all right walking?" The colour had returned to his face, and he was once more the competent head warden with a task to perform.

Rose felt like a good walk after the arduous journey, and she set off with Julius and the gardener. As they walked, she discovered that Aureus Lodge was built on top of an escarpment with spectacular views over Borana, Lewa and on towards Samburu.

When she turned back to look at the lodge, she could also see the three most prominent peaks of Mount Kenya.

Following Kennedy, they scrambled down a rocky slope onto a smaller ridge and from that down onto the valley floor. At the edge of the slope, partially hidden by a small Egyptian thorn tree, was a dusty black hole.

Julius dropped to his knees, sniffed the air, and as he shuffled forward his head and shoulders disappeared from view.

He re-emerged with particles of sand caught in his curly black hair. He stood and brushed the earth from his trousers. "The den is empty, and it looks dry and intact. What do you think?"

Rose looked around at the sparse landscape of Maasai grass, white hibiscus bushes and the occasional umbrella thorn acacia tree. It was now hot in the late morning and she knew that most animals would be resting down their burrows and dens, or in the shade of trees and bushes.

"It appears sheltered and secluded, and as it's not too far from the lodge, someone, perhaps Kennedy here, could monitor the jackals. What is your plan for releasing them?"

Julius paced across from the hole to a small thicket of lyceum bushes and white thorn acacias. "Borana have agreed to build a small enclosure, close to the den, into which we can release them. Do you think this is a good place? Is there enough shade."

Rose wandered towards him. "Yes, I think it will do. I suggest you keep the enclosure closed, and their cages open to start with, until they are comfortable with their environment."

"And then when they are happy, open the enclosure?" Julius asked.

Rose walked back towards the den. "That would be my recommendation. I think you will have to see what happens after that. And whether they immediately take to the den or return to their cages to sleep."

Julius joined her. "Kennedy tells me you're staying this weekend, so he has offered me a room in the staff quarters. If I can arrange transport, and the enclosure can be built in time, we could begin the jackals' rehabilitation this weekend, when we are both here."

Rose clasped her hands together and announced, "That's a great idea."

CHAPTER ELEVEN

R ose removed an attractive peacock coloured skirt from a narrow wooden wardrobe. She rarely dressed up, but she thought she might need something smarter for supper at the lodge. It was Thursday morning and she and Craig were preparing to leave for their weekend away at Borana.

Chris had agreed to try to be civil with his father and was helping by packing Craig's belongings into a small grey suitcase. He laid a green checked shirt on the bed and began to fold it.

Craig was lying on the bed, propped up against the headboard. He snapped, "Don't you know how to fold a shirt properly?"

Oh dear, thought Rose. He's being deliberately difficult. It's probably because Chris has refused to join us at the lodge.

"Dad, I was in the army for fourteen years." Chris kept his voice level. "And we did learn to fold shirts. Perhaps you will allow me to get on with it." Chris raised his head and looked at Rose, smiling. He had been for a long run this morning on Mount Kenya, and the endorphins still seemed to be having a positive effect.

He reached into the wardrobe next to his mother and removed two tweed jackets which he held up, side by side. "Which one do you think?" he asked.

Rose picked at the pocket of one jacket and realised it had a hole in it. Was it worth having the jacket mended? She chided herself. She mustn't think like that. "Not this one, as it has a hole in it. Can you leave it out and I'll see if Kipto can repair it?"

Chris placed the damaged jacket over the back of a chair and the other on the bed.

Rose asked brightly, "So are you staying here when we're away?"

Chris searched through the items he had already packed and answered, "Yes, I will tonight, but tomorrow I'm catching a lift to Lewa and staying in the tented camp BATUK have set up. Then I'll be ready, with my teammates, for the early start on Saturday morning."

Rose turned to Craig. "Should we drive to the start on Saturday? I've never actually been, as we're always positioned out on the course at our water stop. It could be fun to see everyone, especially Chris and Chloe. Although it'll mean an early start."

Craig attempted to lean forward and his eyes softened. "Great idea. And I'm delighted Thabiti has decided to take part with Marina."

CHAPTER TWELVE

Later that afternoon, Rose parked Craig's Subaru at the rear of Aureus Lodge. She had driven steadily through the Ngare Ndare forest, but was still a little concerned because she had heard scraping metal from underneath the car a couple of times as she negotiated particularly deteriorated sections of the road.

Marina rushed forward and threw her arms around Rose. "Isn't this exciting? We are officially open and you are our first guests."

Thabiti was already opening the car boot and removing Craig's wheelchair. He indicated to two African men who hung back. They wore tan-coloured trousers and moss-coloured polo shirts with the lodge emblem across the breast: an acacia tree with a jackal trotting away beneath it.

Rose said, "What about the family's friends. Aren't they here yet?"

Marina bounced on her toes. "They should arrive soon, with Pearl's yoga retreat group. Karanja, the taxi man, is driving them all from Nanyuki."

One of the polo-shirted staff members pushed Craig in his wheelchair. "That must be them," Craig declared. He pointed his arm towards a billowing cloud of dust which was moving towards them.

A smart white people carrier, with a covering of black dust, pulled up next to them. A dapper African man emerged from the driver's seat, smiling broadly. "The couple from Ol Pejeta were delayed, but they won't be long. They're in another of my cars, which is carrying the rest of the luggage."

He slid open the side of the car and three excited women, in their twenties and thirties, emerged and gazed around.

A slightly older lady, with her long dark hair clipped back, stepped out of the car and drawled in an American accent, "Will you look at that? There's a whole lot of scenery."

While Marina welcomed the yoga guests, and led them towards the studio where their classes would be held, Thabiti escorted Rose and Craig towards the central lodge building with its high, steeply sloping, thatched roof.

He said, "We thought it easiest for you to stay in the main part of the house so you're near the dining and drawing rooms. And your bedroom has a fantastic view out over Borana."

Rose asked, "Where are the family friends staying?"

"They're in the other wing of the main house and as the family aren't here, we've split up the yoga party between the smaller rooms at the back of the house, and two of the separate guest buildings. I think Marina wanted as complete a trial as possible of the lodge's facilities and its staff."

Thabiti stopped by a heavy wooden door which he opened to reveal a large proportioned bedroom with a huge double bed, and two wingback chairs positioned by a long window stretching the length of the far wall. Rose stepped closer and realised Thabiti was right. There were fantastic views all the way towards Samburu and beyond.

She turned and admired the combination of elegance and natural elements in the room. The back wall was plastered and painted a soft cream colour, but the other walls were bare, exposing their stone construction.

She looked up and gazed at the high vaulted ceiling with neatly coiled ropes which were the underside of the thatched roof.

They heard raised voices in the corridor.

"But this is not good enough," a man's angry voice sneered. "We are guests of the Edgars', the owners of this lodge, don't you know. I understood we'd have the house to ourselves and that we wouldn't have to share it with any riff-raff."

Thabiti's jaw set as he listened. He turned to Rose and whispered, "We had a call from the Edgars yesterday. This couple, the Scott

Watsons, are not really friends. The Edgars met them recently at a party and felt rather sorry for them. You see, they were coming over here on honeymoon, and were spending the weekend of the Lewa Marathon in the large tented village. That's where the marathon runners who don't have private accommodation stay."

He scowled and scuffed his foot along the floor. "I hate arrogant, self-important people."

CHAPTER THIRTEEN

A flustered Marina joined Rose, Craig, and Thabiti in Rose's large bedroom.

She rubbed her wrists and said politely, "I'm sorry about the noise. I hope the other guests didn't disturb you." She bit her lip and looked down at the floor.

Rose stepped across, laid an arm around Marina's shoulder and said, "We are your friends. You don't have to apologise to us. Anyway, Thabiti explained that the lodge owners offered these guests accommodation out of sympathy. They should be grateful and not throw their weight around and upset you."

Marina ran a hand through her glossy black hair. "And yet he's so pompous. And his poor wife didn't utter a word. I can't say I envy her."

Marina wandered across to the window and stared through it. She breathed in and out deeply three times and then turned to them with a relieved smile.

"What I had been eager to tell you is that we are having a special dinner tonight to mark the opening of the lodge. All the guests will be eating together and we'll be joining you." Marina paused and scratched her neck as she looked in Thabiti's direction.

He shoved his hands into his pockets and stared at the rug covering the wooden floor. Rose felt the tension between Marina and Thabiti. Thabiti was fearful of social situations and particularly worried about meeting and speaking to new people.

In Nanyuki, around people he was getting to know, he was improving, but his anxiety about meeting the other guests, who were strangers to him, was tangible.

Marina swallowed and continued, "There will be cocktails and sundowners by the pool from six o'clock. I hope you can both join us."

Craig reached up and tapped Thabiti on the arm. "I don't think I can manage a full-blown dinner and it will be too tiring with all those people. Would you mind joining me for a light supper in this lovely room?"

Thabiti removed his other hand from his pocket and ran a finger along one arm of the wheelchair.

Rose jumped in. "What a good idea, Craig. There's no point exhausting yourself on the first night, or you might be too tired to enjoy the rest of the weekend."

She turned to Marina. "You don't mind if Thabiti and Craig miss the main dinner, do you?" She looked at Thabiti, whose head was bowed. "Is that OK with you, Thabiti?"

He glanced up at Marina with anguished eyes and quickly returned his attention to the wheelchair.

Marina slapped her thigh. "I agree, that's an excellent idea. But you'll still join us, won't you Rose?" Her forehead wrinkled.

Rose rested a hand on Marina's arm. "Of course, my dear, I'm looking forward to it."

"Good, good." Marina strode across and opened the door. She turned and called, "See you ALL tonight for sundowners."

Thabiti collapsed in one of the wingback chairs. He was sweating. "Thanks for getting me out of that. I don't think I could have coped with all those people and a formal dinner. Marina knows I hate these events, so why did she assume I'd attend?"

Rose sat down opposite him. "She's in her work mode now, trying to run the lodge efficiently, whilst being polite to the guests. And as she's hosting tonight's dinner, she probably assumed you'd join her. She's clearly put an enormous amount of work into setting up the lodge for today's opening. Maybe she just wanted to share her achievement with you."

Thabiti picked at a loose thread on the arm of the chair. "I suppose so. And it looks like I'll have to join you for sundowners."

"You stick with me," declared Craig. "Pushing my wheelchair can be your excuse for not having to mingle."

Thabiti pushed Craig's wheelchair through a gap in the stone wall, onto a paved flagstone area leading to a kidney-shaped swimming pool. Rose followed and looked around in wonder. Trees, shrubs and the stone wall surrounded the secluded pool area.

At the far end was a small thatched building which she presumed was the pool house containing changing rooms, toilets and showers. As she followed Craig and Thabiti, Rose realised that one side of the pool was open, providing an unrestricted view of Borana Conservancy.

In the dimming light she looked east towards the Nyambeni Hills behind which was Meru National Park.

Pearl, Thabiti's sister, was talking with a lean looking Indian man who Rose presumed was the yoga instructor, Ajay. Pearl had suffered terrible depression and stopped eating after her mother's death.

Rose was delighted to see her engaging in yoga and venturing away from home on the retreat. Hopefully this was the first step in her healing process and, perhaps, a step towards independence after being reliant on, and subservient to, her over-protective mother.

The three young women she had seen emerge from Karanja's car giggled close by, and the American woman was talking loudly and animatedly with a dark-haired man. He turned his handsome face and Rose recognised him as the honeymooning husband who'd disembarked from the same flight as Chris the previous Saturday at Nanyuki airstrip.

She thought his name was Robert and that his young wife was called Nina. Rose looked around and spotted her, partly hidden by a flowering cherry tree, on the far side of the swimming pool, gazing eastwards at the view.

Marina was directing staff as they lit candles in coloured paper bags and turned on the lanterns which hung from some of the stronger tree branches. It created the delightful effect of a fairy glade.

Rose plucked a glass of something sparkling from a waiter's tray and wandered across to join Nina.

"Hi, I'm Rose. I saw you at Nanyuki Airstrip last Saturday. How was your visit to Ol Pejeta?"

Nina turned to Rose with wide eyes and said in a soft voice, "It was amazing. There were so many animals. I never dreamt I'd ever get a chance to see them all." She looked across at her husband with parted lips, but quickly looked away, biting her thumbnail.

Frowning, Rose turned towards Robert whose hand was cupping the pert bottom of the American lady. Their heads drew together in what looked like an intimate conversation.

Rose grabbed Nina's arm and towed her unwillingly across the flagstones to Robert and the American lady. She thrust her hand forward so the couple had to part. "Hello I'm Rose. I was just asking your wife if she is enjoying her honeymoon."

The American lady blushed and looked away.

"I say," uttered Robert, "It's frightfully rude interrupting someone's private conversation."

"Well, I think its frightfully rude flirting with another woman when on your honeymoon."

She heard giggles behind her from the yoga women.

Just then, Marina announced loudly and clearly, "Dinner in ten minutes."

"I'm going to freshen up," declared Robert and left the poolside, dragging a shaking Nina with him.

The American lady joined Pearl and Ajay.

Rose pounded across to Craig and Thabiti. Thabiti's head was turned away. He glanced at her with his hand covering his mouth, but quickly turned away again as he began to shake with laughter.

Rose could feel the warmth in her cheeks and the blood pounding in her chest. Craig grabbed her hand. "Well done, old thing. But I'd rather you didn't repeat the performance. That man looked very angry, as if he wanted to punish someone. I don't want that person to be you."

"Hmm," murmured Rose as she looked towards the main building with pursed lips. "I've learnt my lesson about ignoring bullying husbands. If I see one mark on that poor girl, I will have it out with him."

Craig tightened his grip. "Steady on."

Marina appeared beside them, wearing a stunning red satin dress.

She grabbed Rose's arm and pulled her to one side and whispered, "Will you help me with the seating plan? I don't want to cause any further upset."

Craig looked up at Thabiti, who had now composed himself. "I think we've done our duty. Shall we retire to my room for supper?"

CHAPTER FOURTEEN

R ose and Julius stood by a small wire-
fenced enclosure near the empty jackal
den, at the base of the escarpment on Borana
Conservancy.

"What do you think?" asked Julius.

"It looks good to me." She shook the metre-high
fence. "Safe and secure, and those white thorn
acacia trees will provide plenty of shade during
the day."

It was half past ten and already Rose could feel
the heat from the sun on her head. She was
relieved she'd remembered to bring a small,

floppy, wide-brimmed hat with her as it also protected her eyes from the glare of the sun.

"Shall we get started?" she asked, and they moved across to two safari vehicles which the Mount Kenya Resort and Spa had kindly lent them to move the jackals. Julius had also brought four of his orphanage staff, who gingerly lifted large plastic crates out of the back of the cars.

"Your friend Dr Emma found us the crates. They've been lent to us by British Army families who brought their dogs with them when they were posted to the training base in Nanyuki."

He moved towards two of his staff. "Stand at each end of the crate and lift it. Rather than one of you walking backwards, turn around so you are both walking sideways," he instructed. He stepped back as they lifted the crate.

"Steady, keep it level, and no jerky movements. The jackals will be worried enough after their long bumpy journey."

Rose and Julius shut the enclosure gate and stood outside, watching as the cages were opened. One jackal emerged.

"That's the male one," commented Julius.

"How do you know?"

"We were going to fit them with GPS tracking collars, but they were too bulky, so after we weighed each of them, back at the orphanage, we shaved a different shaped area of hair on their bottoms so we can quickly identify them."

"What a clever idea."

Rose watched two more jackals emerge to explore their surroundings, whilst the fourth remained in its crate.

CHAPTER FIFTEEN

At half past four, Rose joined her fellow guests on the wooden viewing deck outside the drawing room. Craig had chosen to forgo the evening activities and watch the sunset from their room.

Thabiti had taken him for a short drive earlier, and he was excited by the solar energy solutions that the conservancy was working on.

Marina walked out onto the viewing deck, followed by Thabiti and a stocky African man.

"Are we all here?" she asked, looking around the group. "We're just missing Robert and

Nina." She clasped her hands together. "Not to worry. They have requested a driving safari tonight, rather than joining you on your game walk with Reuben."

She stepped aside and indicated to the stocky man, who stepped forward and nodded towards the group.

Marina continued, "Reuben is in charge of the tracker dogs at Lewa Conservancy and has extensive knowledge of both Lewa and Borana Conservancies, and their flora and fauna."

One of the yoga ladies piped up, "Can we drive round as well rather than walk?"

Marina turned to Thabiti, who shrugged. She replied, "Yes, of course. Just give us five minutes to prepare one of the larger vehicles."

"I'll go," murmured Thabiti, and he turned to leave the room. He jumped back quickly as Robert strode through the door with Nina running to catch up with him.

"I hope we didn't miss anything," he drawled.

Marina smiled at him. "Not at all. Thabiti was just leaving to prepare the vehicle for your game drive with the ladies."

"What ladies?" he snarled.

"Us," the yoga girls chorused, and stepped past him, laughing.

Reuben led his small party down a winding path in a north-westerly direction, away from the lodge. Rose followed Reuben, picking her way over protruding rocks and being careful not to slip in the loose, sandy soil.

"I do hope there aren't any snakes," shrilled the American lady behind her, whose name she had discovered was Wendy.

They reached the bottom of the slope and turned towards the north-west. Pearl and Thabiti joined Rose, and they walked side-by-side. Wendy was in front with Reuben.

Pearl had an aura of self-assurance which Rose had not witnessed before. She strode along with strong powerful strides but also an elegant suppleness. In her all black outfit, with a bright yellow scarf around her neck, she reminded Rose of a cheetah loping across the savannah.

"How is the yoga retreat?" Rose asked her.

"Not bad." Pearl stepped around a white hibiscus bush. "The girls are a bit giggly during the group session, but there's an instructor from Lewa coming over tomorrow. He's going to teach Wendy and myself some more Zujitsu."

Thabiti, who was walking with his hands in his pockets, queried, "I thought it was called Jujitsu?"

"It is, that's to say, the Japanese martial art is. Zujitsu was developed in America by a man called Chaka Zulu. He's blended his African heritage of fighting rhythms and dancing with street fighting styles and self-defence. You need to be really fit to complete his routines."

Reuben stopped and squatted on the ground. He picked up a stick and pointed it at a column of very large ants. "You have fire ants in America, I think?" he looked up at Wendy.

"Yes, horrible stinging creatures." Wendy shivered.

"Well, these are driver ants. And they're far worse, so don't step on them."

Thabiti peered at the small creatures scurrying along, carrying small twigs and leaves. "Aren't those siafu?"

Reuben stood up. "Yes, that's what we call them."

Thabiti leapt back. "They're vicious. I remember when I was young and we were at a wedding with my parents. Everyone was sitting on straw bales and suddenly sprang up and started dancing about. I thought it was all part of the celebration until I felt a sharp nip on my thigh."

He looked at his sister. "Do you remember? Mum had to lift your skirt and bat them off your legs."

"Oh, yes," laughed Pearl. "And she had to take your socks and trousers off, and she even found one of the siafu in your underpants."

Pink spots appeared on Thabiti's cheeks.

Pearl burst out laughing. "It would have been embarrassing for you, but for Aunt Delilah. She was hopping around, making such a fuss that other members of the congregation tore her dress off and she continued bouncing her well-proportioned body around in a purple bra and knickers."

Wendy stepped gingerly over the ants, and they continued their walk.

Thabiti appeared deep in thought, and every so often he kicked at a stone.

"What's bothering you?" Rose asked gently.

"That's the last thing we did with Pa. People said he stole the money from the church that day and did a runner, but Ma refused to talk about it."

"Well, I'm not surprised," responded Pearl.

"Shh." Wendy turned to them and pointed at a large black and white bird with long legs and a series of feather quills protruding from its head.

They watched it stride across the grass in front of them.

"It's a secretary bird," Reuben said. "They like these grassland areas."

Wendy asked, "Can it fly? It looks as if it's almost too big to fly."

"They can, but flapping their wings is rather laborious and takes a lot of energy. If you spook one, it's likely to take flight for a short distance and then land and continue on foot."

As they walked on, Thabiti asked Pearl, "What are you not surprised about?"

"That Ma refused to talk about Pa. Not only did he embarrass her by stealing money her family had donated to the church, and to whichever cousin or second-cousin was getting married, but he also stole from her."

Pearl clenched her fists. "And it wasn't only money. He took some of her mother's jewellery, which Grandad had only recently given her."

They emerged by the side of a watering hole surrounded by clumps of sedges. At the far side, a herd of female impala were drinking at the water's edge, while their male leader restlessly kept guard behind them.

"Follow me," Reuben told them. He led them around the side of the watering hole until they emerged onto a wooden platform. Folded wooden safari chairs were propped against a rail on one side of the platform. Reuben opened one and positioned it at the front of the viewing platform for Wendy.

Thabiti helped set up more chairs and he, Pearl and Rose sat a little distance away from Wendy and Reuben.

Thabiti tapped the arm of his chair. "I don't remember anything about that."

Pearl gave him a pitying look, but one which held a mixture of nostalgia and sympathy. "You were young and couldn't understand why Pa wasn't around to play football with you."

Pearl sat back and knitted her hands together. "Looking back, I'm not sure whether Pa left of his own accord, or whether Ma kicked him out. She certainly threatened to do so on more than one occasion. I remember them arguing, and it seemed that he was always involved in some scheme or other to make a lot of money. Of course he never did."

"So he was what you'd call 'a chancer'." Thabiti looked glum.

"I'm afraid so," agreed Pearl.

Thabiti's thoughts were interrupted as Wendy cried out, "Oh, look, elephants."

CHAPTER SIXTEEN

R ose heard a car engine, and a few minutes later Marina and a member of the lodge staff stepped onto the platform carrying a folded table and a cool box. They erected the table and the staff member collected another cool box from the car. Marina shook a red Kanga cloth and placed it over the table.

She approached Rose, Thabiti and Pearl and asked, "How was your bush walk? Did you see anything exciting?"

Wendy turned in her chair and exclaimed, "Oh yeah. We've just seen ourselves a mighty herd of elephants."

"A group of about five with a young baby came down to the waterhole," explained Rose.

"I'll just get set up for sundowners. The car with the other guests should be here shortly," Marina said, and gave Thabiti a deliberate look as she moved back to the table.

Rose tapped Thabiti on the leg. "You should help Marina. You are being paid by the lodge now, and she can't do everything on her own. Besides, I think you will find it more comfortable fixing drinks than talking with the guests."

Thabiti glanced nervously behind him as they heard another car approach. He stood and set up the remaining chairs before joining Marina.

The giggling yoga women danced onto the platforms and with oohs and aahs. They pulled three chairs to the edge of the platform and began pointing as a family of warthogs appeared and warily approached the watering hole.

"I'll have a large gin and tonic, boy. Tanqueray if you have it." Rose turned around and saw that Robert was addressing Thabiti.

Thabiti had his head bowed, but Rose could see that his mouth was set in a thin, hard line.

Nina stood behind Thabiti's empty chair and asked timidly, "Do you mind if I sit down?"

Rose patted the seat, "Do join us and tell us all about your game drive. Borana is quite incredible, isn't it?"

Nina relaxed and her eyes sparkled. "To start with, I didn't think we'd see much, and then we turned a corner and there was a rhino, with its baby." She whispered, "And we were able to drive quite close."

Marina moved amongst the guests and ensured everyone had a drink. As the light dimmed, they watched birds, antelope and a giraffe all drink at the watering hole.

Marina stood to one side and announced, "If I could have your attention for a few minutes so we can run through tomorrow's itinerary."

A hush descended over the group.

"As some of you know," Marina continued, "tomorrow is the famous Lewa Marathon. Robert and Nina, you will be leaving with Thabiti and I at six-thirty am. There will be a light breakfast set up in the dining room from six."

She turned to the yoga women. "A full breakfast will be served in the dining room from seven until eight. And your lunch will be provided by the pool, as it was today."

"That sounds just perfect," shrilled Wendy.

Marina joined Rose's group. "What are your and Craig's plans for tomorrow?"

"We'd like to come to the marathon and support you all." She turned to Nina. "Have you competed in any marathons before?"

Nina looked down and rubbed her wrist. "We're only running the half marathon. I've completed a few 10K races at home. This will be much more challenging, but I have been training. I was very careful to follow a set programme so I undertook the right amount of running without getting injured."

"And your husband?" inquired Pearl.

"Oh, he doesn't need to do so much. He's a natural athlete, unlike me."

She shuffled her feet and knocked over her glass. Jumping up, she cried, "Silly me."

Marina patted her shoulder. "Don't worry." She picked up the fallen glass. "The wood will soak up whatever has been spilt. Sit back down and I'll fetch you another drink."

Pearl asked Nina, "Is this your first trip to Africa?"

Nina nervously sipped the drink Marina handed her and then clutched the glass. "I've visited South Africa before, but nothing like this. We always take a suite in one of the upmarket hotels, which has good business facilities so Daddy can keep in touch with work. And Mummy would hate being in the bush, as there are too many insects and not enough shops."

Rose placed a hand on her leg. "But you're enjoying it, aren't you? And are you happy?"

"Oh, yes." She looked across at Robert who had joined Wendy and Reuben and her voice cracked as she said, "I'm so lucky to have Robert. We moved to the country when I was twelve, but Mummy and Daddy still spend a lot of time in London. We are what people call nouveau riche, and because my parents still speak with native London accents, I don't get invited to many parties."

Pearl asked, "So how did you meet Robert?"

"At Ascot, at the races." Her eyes shone. "I love horses, which is why I went with Mummy and Daddy. Normally I find those things so dull, but the horses' coats were gleaming, and the racing was really exciting. Robert was in the neighbouring box. He came out onto the balcony and saw me standing alone, so he started talking to me. I just thought he felt sorry for me, but a year later we married."

Thabiti and a member of staff started clearing the table.

Marina said to Rose. "Will you drive across to the marathon in the morning in your own car? You could come with us, but I'm not sure how long we'll be. And what do you want to do about breakfast?"

Rose stood so Thabiti could fold away her chair. "I thought I would grab something from the breakfast table. Could someone in the kitchen prepare a flask of hot water with some tea, coffee and milk?"

Marina nudged her arm playfully. "We can do better than that. I'll ask the kitchen to prepare you a proper picnic breakfast and some sandwiches in case you stay longer."

CHAPTER SEVENTEEN

Early on Saturday morning, Rose followed Thabiti, who was driving one of the lodge's safari vehicles, between vertical banners proclaiming the Lewa Marathon. Thabiti was directed to the competitors' car park, and an official flagged Rose down.

She opened the window and said, "My husband is disabled. Is there anywhere closer we can park?"

The official ducked down and looked into the car at her and Craig before tearing off a blue ticket. "Here, put this under your windscreen. Continue until you reach Dormans' coffee van. Then turn left and follow a track which will take you up beyond the start to the first water stop."

Rose crawled along in the dim light. Her arthritic fingers were sore and throbbed from the effort of winding the window and clutching the steering wheel in the chill early morning.

She leant forward, peering out of the windscreen as she tried to make sure she didn't knock down one of the competitors as they made their way to the start.

She turned left and picked up speed as the number of people dwindled. She found a flat area to park and turned the car so they had a good view of the starting line, which was marked by a large overhead banner.

The competitors would run along the brown soil track in front of them, which wound its way up a hill and away into Lewa Conservancy.

Craig looked around and said, "This is perfect. I can see what's going on without being bothered by people or jostled by the crowd. Do you want to go and see who's taking part?"

She turned to him, "Do you mind?"

"Not at all. Can you pour me a cup of coffee first? And then you can tell me who you saw when you get back."

Rose prepared Craig's coffee and arranged a green woollen rug over his legs.

She wandered back down the track and picked her way across the dry bamboo grass towards the competitors.

The first group she came across were some of her fellow East African Women's League members who were all over sixty. They greeted her warmly as they bounced up and down on the soles of their feet, which she suspected was to keep them warm rather than being in preparation for the marathon ahead.

The crowd parted as a group of fit looking men and women, wearing khaki green t-shirts, marched towards the start line and the front of the crowd of runners.

They were the British army team from BATUK, and Rose spotted Chris amongst them. As if he could feel her gaze, he turned and smiled at her. She mouthed "Good luck."

The next group she met were a shivering bunch of African runners from one of the local flower farms. She knew some of them by sight, as she visited the farm regularly to check the health and welfare of the security dogs. She called, "Bahati njema," to them.

They responded with, "Asanti, Mama Rose."

At the far side of the assembled runners, standing at the back, were Marina, Robert and Nina.

Nina shivered and rubbed her hands down her bare arms. Over a black t-shirt she wore a distinctive pink vest which announced, 'Breast Cancer Awareness'.

Rose presumed the figure standing apart from the group, wearing a black beanie hat on his bowed head, was Thabiti.

"Good luck, Thabiti. And enjoy your walk," called Chloe as she jogged past him and joined Rose, Marina, Robert and Nina.

Robert's eyes ran their way up and down Chloe and he leaned back, smiling in satisfaction. She wore a distinctive pink and light blue top with 'Baby Loss Awareness' written across it, and number '487' in large black lettering stuck to her back.

"Isn't this exciting?" Chloe looked around the burgeoning crowd of runners, but her eyes were dull and she picked at her running top.

"Where's Dan?" Rose asked.

Chloe continued to fiddle with her top. "He wanted to run with his army mates."

Marina engulfed her in a brief hug. "Don't worry, you'll be fine. Go out and show him how good you are, girl."

Chloe's lips began to curl upwards into a faint smile. She touched Marina on the arm and said, "Thanks, I will."

The two young women maintained eye contact and Marina stated simply, "Good luck".

"And you," responded Chloe as she turned to look at Thabiti, who was kicking at a kei apple bush. "And I'm sure he'll be fine once you set off."

Marina raised her eyes to the sky and shook her head. "He's been complaining all morning."

"I'm going to try to get a spot closer to the start," Chloe stated. "But I'll wait for you both at the finishing line. Bye, Rose," she called as she threaded her way through the other runners who were also beginning to surge towards the starting line.

"Come on," said Robert, grabbing Nina's arm. He pulled her after Chloe, but their way was soon barred by the sheer number of people. Rose watched Robert raise his head and peer around as if trying to find an alternative route. He stopped and stared at someone or something.

Rose followed the direction of his gaze and thought she spotted the brunette head of the lady who'd flown in from Lewa, when they were lunching at Barney's, but the figure vanished and she couldn't be sure.

Thabiti slouched towards them. "This is so embarrassing. My time on the finishing board will be so slow compared with everyone else," he moaned.

Rose pursed her lips. "How do they time everyone? Do they use safari clocks? It must be difficult at the finishing line if groups of competitors run through together."

Thabiti looked up. "They only use stopwatches to check the winners of the elite races. Nowadays the timing is automated and done by transponder chips."

He tore off his paper number, turned it over and pointed at a second piece of paper on the reverse side. "See that length of white plastic?"

Rose nodded as she spotted an inch long piece of translucent plastic, attached to the paper, with a bar code beneath it.

"That's a passive transponder, and it sends a unique code that is detected by radio receivers. I'm not sure if there is a receiver at the start or if we are all given the same starting time. But at the end it will tell the judges how long it has taken to complete the course. And that is the competitor's finishing time."

He handed his number to Marina. "Can you stick this back on for me?"

"Welcome, everyone," a male voice boomed, and they turned to listen to a middle-aged man, standing on a platform next to the start. "Are there any more elite runners? You have numbers with a red background."

Rose saw the sea of runners sway and presumed people were pushing their way to the front.

The man with the microphone spoke again. "Watch the clock. Only one more minute to go." A large digital clock attached to the banner counted down.

The man shouted, "Ten, nine, eight."

Rose felt the tension amongst the competitors.

Marina grabbed Thabiti's arm. "Let's go." She called over her shoulder to Rose, "See you at the finish."

Rose's reply of "Enjoy yourselves" was lost in the shouts and cries from the runners as the man shouted "GO".

Rose followed the final competitors as they streamed towards the starting line. She looked up the track which was packed with runners and reminded her of the siafu ants they had found on their bush walk. She felt weary and her gnarled fingers ached. It wasn't that long ago, was it, that she would have been out there, relishing the challenge of the marathon.

"Mama Rose," a voice called.

She turned as a giant of an African man sauntered towards her. He was surprisingly light on his feet, considering his size. She recognised her friend, Sam Mwamba, an officer of the Kenya Wildlife Service (KWS) member of the Elite Kenyan Anti-poaching unit.

He had the unerring habit of appearing whenever there was trouble.

Sam cocked his head to one side. "What's up? Aren't you happy to see me?"

She realised she was scowling. "Sorry, Sam, of course I am. I'm just concerned that your appearance is a warning of perils ahead."

Sam laughed. "Surely not. I'm just helping with the technical side of the marathon. What about you? Are you on your own?"

"Craig's with me, but he's struggling to get around at the moment. I parked the car up there so he could watch the start." She turned and pointed towards the lone Subaru. "We're staying with Marina and Thabiti at the new lodge they're managing on Borana. The owners cried off from the marathon, but they offered their places to Marina and Thabiti. So I came to wish them luck."

Sam placed his hands on his hips and grinned. "I thought I spotted Thabiti hiding under a beanie cap. And I saw your friend Chloe begin with a determined expression on her face. Did you bump into Judy before the start?"

Rose's mind went blank.

"Judy. Constable Wachira?" Sam repeated.

"Oh, your Judy."

Sam shuffled his feet.

"No. I didn't. Is she running the half marathon?"

Sam pinned his shoulders back and smiled proudly. "She's running the full marathon with some colleagues of mine from the KWS."

Rose started. "Wow, that's quite an undertaking. I hope she'll be OK."

"She'll be just fine. She's a competent runner, and she's fit and determined. Now if you'll excuse me, I need to check my equipment at the finishing line."

CHAPTER EIGHTEEN

After the race started, Rose returned to Craig. She reversed the Subaru back onto the track and decided to drive along and see how far it went. It appeared to continue on a course roughly parallel with that of the runners. A smaller track branched right, and at the end of it she spotted what she presumed was the first water stop.

They drove over the crest of a hill and Craig proclaimed, "Now isn't that an amazing sight!"

Below them was a bobbing, swaying river of runners stretching out in a line as far as they could see.

The track finished by another water stop and Rose parked by a bend in the running track to ensure that Craig could see the runners from the car.

"I'm going to stretch my legs and see who I can spot," she told Craig as she extracted herself from the driver's seat.

A group of green-topped runners ran past, but Chris was not amongst them.

The water stop was sponsored by Highlands Water, and the staff handing out water and branded sodas wore white t-shirts with the company name printed in bold blue letters.

Rose stood to one side and watched as runners ran or walked up to the wooden trestle table. Some stopped, but the majority grabbed hold of the plastic glasses and drank their water as they ran along the track.

She tutted as she watched them carelessly discard their empty glasses into the grass beside the path.

The Highlands water stop team would have to collect the plastic glasses, and from previous experience, Rose knew how hard this job was in the heat of the late morning sun.

A group of runners crowded around the table, and Rose spotted Chloe's blue and pink top. She thought she recognised another face behind Chloe, but before she had time to process the image, there was a kerfuffle and Chloe was pushed onto the table into the plastic glasses which spilt water everywhere.

"Hey, careful. There's no need to push," cried Chloe.

Chloe shuffled along the table until she had some space where she brushed herself down.

Rose rushed over and asked, "Are you OK? What happened?"

Chloe looked up with cold eyes and a curled lip. "Someone slapped me on the back and pushed me into the table. I'm soaked." She held out the bottom of her running top.

"As long as you're OK, I wouldn't worry about that. It'll soon dry and you might be relieved by the cooling effect of the water evaporating."

Chloe looked at her and back at the table, now restocked with fresh water glasses. She grinned as a runner grabbed a glass and poured the water over his head rather than drinking it. His face was bright red, and he was gasping for air.

"No harm done," Chloe assured Rose. "But I better keep going. I was maintaining an excellent position, just behind the main army group." She looked down at her feet. "I want to prove I can run just as well as Dan's mates."

Chloe set off energetically down the track.

As Rose watched, Robert and Nina ran past. They'd done well to catch up, she thought.

CHAPTER NINETEEN

T habiti still wasn't sure why he'd agreed to run in the Lewa Marathon. Not that this could be called running. They were being forced to walk by the sheer number of people around them.

He looked ahead as one competitor broke away from the pack and overtook the line of people by running along the grass beside the path. Ahead, he could see the bright pink top of Nina Scott Watson.

Some runners, who wore white tops with green and red sleeves, stopped in front of them at the first water stop. He and Marina skirted around them and found the path ahead clearer.

Marina commented, "Nina and Robert are quite quick now they have space to run. Shall we jog along for a while?"

As his muscles warmed up, he found it easier to run, especially once the path reached the summit of a small hill and they began a steady descent.

As they approached the third water stop, he heard Craig's voice shout, "Well done, keep going."

Looking about, he spotted the Subaru parked by a bend in the track and Craig in the passenger seat with the door open. Thabiti waved as they ran past.

"Let's stop here," panted Marina. "There's another half kilometre of flat ground before we start a steep climb."

She grabbed a plastic cup of water from the wooden trestle table, handed it to Thabiti and took another for herself. They moved away from the group gathered around the table and sipped their water.

"Wow, look at the skyline along the top of that hill." Marina pointed excitedly. "I can see two giraffes silhouetted against it."

Mama Rose joined them and asked, "Everything OK?"

Thabiti nodded as Marina pointed to the dark shapes of the giraffes against the orange-tinted sky.

"It's amazing, isn't it?" Mama Rose commented. "Where else in the world could you organise a running race with no barriers between the wildlife and competitors."

Marina asked, "Have you seen anyone else come past?"

Rose nodded. "We were too late to see Chris and his army mates, but arrived just in time to see Chloe. There must have been a scuffle for water as someone bumped into her and pushed her onto the table."

"Is she OK?" Marina asked in a concerned voice.

"She's fine. Just a little put out, I think. And a little wet from the water that was spilt on her." Rose stared up the track as competitors ran, jogged, and strode purposefully past. "And Nina and Robert weren't far behind." More people passed them. "You better keep going before you get too cold and stiff."

Thabiti looked at Marina and they jogged on.

CHAPTER TWENTY

Rose and Craig drove on towards the finishing area of the Lewa Marathon. A group of five lean African runners ran past in the opposite direction.

"They'll be running the full marathon and heading out on their second lap. And they're going at quite a pace. You know they don't look the least bit tired," commented Craig.

"How long do you think it'll be before they overtake the back markers of the half marathon?" asked Rose. She could now see the large finishing banner ahead of them.

"I think it's usually around the halfway point," replied Craig. "The fastest runners complete the marathon in less than two and a half hours."

Rose braked to a stop and watched two men sprint down the finishing funnel, around the corner and towards the finishing line.

"That's quick for completing the half marathon," declared Craig. "I make it one hour six minutes."

Rose parked Craig's Subaru behind a line of white tents with pointed roofs. She turned to Craig. "I'll find someone to help you into your wheelchair, and then we can have our picnic breakfast whilst we cheer home the runners."

She looked at her watch. "I can't believe it's only quarter to nine, but I suppose we were up early."

Rose found a strong young man with the Amref team, who were providing medical cover for the event, to help Craig.

"Thank you," she said and wheeled Craig to a shaded area, ten metres in front of the finishing line. They had an unobstructed view of the runners as they rounded the final bend to complete the full and half marathons. She returned to the car and collected a soft cool bag, a basket, and a rug to sit on.

"Please can you pour me a coffee?" asked Craig. "And tell me, what treats do we have for breakfast?"

Rose opened the cool bag and peered inside. "Oh, wonderful." She pulled out a glass jar layered with granola, fresh berries and yoghurt.

Craig pressed his lips together as he examined the granola jar. "Is there anything else?"

Rose lifted out a smaller insulated bag. She unzipped it and unwrapped the foil inside.

Craig licked his lips. "That's more like it. It smells delicious."

Rose handed him a plate with a still warm, home-made English muffin, filled with scrambled egg and crispy bacon.

The smell was so enticing that she also began to eat one.

"Here come the first European runners," Craig announced as he turned his head. "And the clock at the finish says one hour thirty-five minutes."

They continued their breakfast and watched more finishers, who were predominantly African men. There were a few African women, a handful of European men, and Rose was pleased to see the first two European women complete the half marathon.

Craig tapped her on the shoulder. "Here come the first BATUK finishers. That's good, they've run as a team." Four green t-shirted runners ran past. Rose stared down the track, seeking out Chris.

She spotted him ten minutes later.

She jumped up and shouted, "Come on, Chris." He and his teammates rounded the bend and sprinted towards the finishing line. They were soon followed by another group of three BATUK runners and then a lone, blonde-haired Chloe.

She started to sprint but slipped as she rounded the turn. The gathering crowd gasped, but she picked herself up and stiffly ran the final twenty metres to the finishing line.

"I'll see if she's OK," Rose told Craig, before weaving as quickly as she could through the swelling crowd. She spotted Chloe sitting on the floor, apart from the other finishers. Her head was bowed over her knees, which she pulled tightly to her chest.

Rose squatted down beside her. "Well done. That was a fantastic run."

Chloe looked up. Her cheeks were flushed and strands of hair were glued to her face with sweat. She pushed them away with her hand and Rose noticed the medal hanging around her neck.

"That's something to be proud of."

"It would be if I hadn't made such an idiot of myself by falling at the last bend."

"Oh, I wouldn't worry about that." Rose reassured her. "I doubt many people will remember, as they will be more concerned about the runners they've come to cheer home. Now I don't want you to catch a chill."

She looked up and saw some runners had kikois wrapped around their shoulders. "I wonder where those came from?"

"They're probably in the goody bag they handed us at the finish." Chloe handed her a cloth bag from which she extracted a pink, green and yellow striped kikoi which she wrapped around Chloe's shoulders.

An attractive-looking man peeled himself away from the group of BATUK competitors. "Have you just finished?" he asked Chloe.

One of the BATUK competitors waved a sheet of paper and shouted to the man, "Hey, Dan, I told you I'd beat you. And you only just beat your wife."

Dan, thought Rose. This must be Chloe's husband. Dan snatched the results sheet and returned to Chloe. As he read the sheet, he rubbed his parted lips with his finger and then looked down at Chloe. "These are the results. They say that you were only two runners behind me, you and another woman."

Chloe struggled to her feet. She stared straight into Dan's surprised face. "I told you I'd been training. I'm going for a post-race massage." She turned and walked towards one of the white tents. Although her back was straight and she held her head high, she moved with short, uneven steps.

Rose turned away from the BATUK runners but was intercepted by Robert. "Hello, was that a friend of yours? Has she just finished?"

Robert was sweating, but seemed remarkably unaffected by the race. "Yes, she finished a few minutes ago. She's stiff from a fall, so she's gone for a massage. How's Nina?"

Robert pointed to another figure sitting hunched on the ground. She had also wrapped the kikoi around her neck and shoulders, over her pink top, and she'd found a baseball cap to cover her head. Robert followed Rose's gaze and commented, "She didn't want to get sunburnt."

Rose realised the day was warming up quickly and as she glanced across at Craig, she realised he was no longer in the shade.

"Thanks for your tip about the massage," said Robert, and strode back to his wife.

Rose searched the group of finishers for Chris. She spotted him and waved.

Chris peeled himself away from his friends and joined her.

"Hi Mum. It was good to see you at the start. I wasn't sure if you would make it. What about Dad? Is he with you?"

Rose placed her hand on her son's arm. "That was a great run. I'm so pleased for you, and I'm actually a little jealous. I was nearly fifty when the first marathon was held and as only teams could enter back then, I never thought about running. Besides, your father and I were asked to help run one of the water stops. You know, he's very proud of you."

"Is he really?" Chris asked. His cheeks coloured, and he looked down at his hands.

"Of course. Come and see him," Rose suggested.

"Chris, are you ready to go?" one of his BATUK teammates shouted.

Chris turned and replied, "Can you give me five minutes?"

"We're going to walk back to camp. See you there in fifteen?"

"OK."

Rose and Chris returned to Craig, who was pink in the face.

Chris rushed forward, grabbed the wheelchair and pulled it back into the shade.

"Thank you," sighed Craig as he tried to lift a trembling hand. "I'm sorry to be a burden to your mother."

Rose took one of Craig's hands in her own and said in an apologetic tone, "You're not a burden. It's my fault. I'm so sorry, I shouldn't have left you sitting in the sun." She began to pack up the picnic bags.

Craig looked up at Chris. "That was a great run. Good for you. Did you find it tiring?"

Chris squatted by his father and answered, "Thanks, Dad. I knew the hills would be hard work, but I hadn't realised quite how long the end section was. I had to push myself to keep up with the boys. And I don't think I have fully acclimatised to the altitude. Still, it's all done now."

Craig lifted a hand weakly and gently rubbed his son's head.

"I've got to get back to camp or I'll miss my lift." Chris patted his father's leg and stood.

Rose hung the cool box and basket from the handles of the wheelchair and laid the rug across them.

Chris gave her a brief hug.

Craig began, "When …"

Rose interrupted and blurted, "Enjoy the rest of the day with your friends."

As Chris walked away, she bent down to Craig and in a soft tone said, "Sorry to cut you off, but I didn't think now was the time to nag him. He'll come and see us when he's ready. For now, let him have time with his friends to celebrate his achievement."

Craig smiled weakly, "Perhaps you're right."

They continued to watch competitors who now appeared in ones and twos. After another fifteen minutes, Rose announced, "Here are Marina and Thabiti."

CHAPTER TWENTY-ONE

Marina and Thabiti jogged towards the finishing line. Rose removed the cool box and basket from the handlebars of Craig's wheelchair, and pushed her way through a throng of excited competitors to join them.

Thabiti was squatting on the ground with the contents of his race goody bag scattered about him.

"Chocolate," he announced in satisfaction. He gathered up the rest of the items and returned them to the bag before unwrapping his chocolate bar. He took a bite, and with a dreamy look on his face, declared, "It was all worthwhile."

Marina grabbed Rose's arm. "We did it. We completed the Lewa Marathon." She lifted the metal medal hanging around her neck. "Look, we've even been given medals to prove it."

"And we weren't last," mused Thabiti.

"I should hope not!" cried Chloe as she bounded up to them. She hugged Marina. "Well done."

Chloe turned to Thabiti.

He stepped back, looking wary of Chloe's hug.

She lowered her arms and said proudly, "And you too, Thabiti."

Marina exclaimed. "When did you finish? You look amazing, as if you're ready to run the whole thing again."

"Not likely," Chloe laughed.

Rose turned to Chloe and said, "You look much better. Did you enjoy your massage?"

Chloe touched Rose's arm. "It was wonderful. And so relaxing that I think I went to sleep for a few minutes."

She leaned back and rubbed her forehead. "There was something strange, though. My number vanished from my running top. It was there when I took it off for my massage, but now it's gone." Chloe turned around, showing her empty back. "And I was going to frame it with my medal." Her shoulders slumped.

"Weird," remarked Marina.

Rose pursed her lips. "Do you think someone sneaked into the tent and took it whilst you were asleep?"

Chloe shivered. "I guess they must have, but why would they want it?"

Marina slapped Chloe on the arm. "Perhaps it was a secret admirer who whisked your number away as a keepsake. Tell me, what was your finishing time?"

Chloe and Marina chatted about their marathon experiences as Thabiti searched through the cool box and removed an egg and bacon muffin.

Rose heard a roar of cheers and applause and turned towards the finishing line. A group of five runners were approaching. Three men and a woman wore green t-shirts with KWS across the front, and with them was the black-clad

Constable Wachira with Police across the front of her shirt.

Rose called to her companions, "Look, here comes Constable Wachira. I saw Sam earlier, and he told me she was running the full marathon."

"That's amazing," cried Marina. "Who is she?"

Thabiti answered. "Sam's girlfriend, although he's surprisingly shy about admitting it. She works at the police station in Nanyuki. And she helped Rose solve Davina Dijan's murder at the Mount Kenya Resort and Spa."

Robert approached Marina. "Nina and I are ready to head back. Where is the lodge car you organised for us?"

"Let me find it for you," replied Marina.

Rose picked up the basket and said, "We parked behind the Amref tent. It might be there as well. I'll show you as I need to put these back in the car."

"Let's look." Marina carried the cool box, and she and Robert followed Rose the short distance to the car. "How was your marathon experience?" she asked Robert.

"Easier than I expected. It all went smoothly. We even saw some wildlife, which Nina particularly enjoyed."

"There's the lodge car," Marina announced, "and Kennedy's driving it." She turned to Rose and said, "We might as well put the breakfast things in Kennedy's car and he can return them to the kitchen."

Marina loaded the cool box and basket into the car whilst Robert searched through a basket which was already in it. He pulled out the floppy wide-brimmed hat with a red bow, which Vivian had given Nina.

"This will be better than a baseball cap to keep the sun off Nina's head. She's starting to develop a headache."

Marina drew her eyebrows together in concern, and asked, "Would you like me to come back with you?"

"No," Robert snapped. In a smoother tone he said, "We'd just like to enjoy a relaxing ride back to the lodge together."

Marina tapped him on the arm and smiled. "Of course, I understand."

Marina and Rose returned to the finishing area. Chloe and Thabiti appeared with Craig, whose wheelchair Thabiti was pushing.

Dan approached Chloe with a tight face and barked, "There you are. I've been looking for you everywhere. I want to head back to Nanyuki. A few of us are going to Kongoni's this afternoon to celebrate. Do you want to come?"

Chloe crossed her arms. "I'll think about it."

She turned to Marina and hugged her. "Well done, and good luck with your guests. Bye," she called to Thabiti and Rose, and ran to catch up with Dan.

Rose heard Robert shout, "See you later," and she turned to watch him and his wife, who had pulled her floppy hat low over her head, leave.

"Would you like a lift back to the start to collect your car?" she asked Marina and Thabiti.

"Yes, please," they chorused.

CHAPTER TWENTY-TWO

R ose had enjoyed a relaxing afternoon sitting on the wooden viewing deck outside the drawing room at Aureus Lodge.

She'd emailed her daughter Heather in the UK and updated her with Chris's performance in the marathon. She'd also added some titbits about the other competitors who Heather knew.

She sighed contentedly and began to flick through a book about the Laikipia Plateau which contained some stunning photographs.

It had been fantastic to see so many people taking part in the marathon, and all the money they raised for wildlife conservation, via the Tusk Trust and Lewa Conservancy. Chris had seemed relaxed and happy with his friends, although she was still concerned that his relationship with Craig remained fragile.

And then there was poor Chloe, who she knew had been trying to accommodate her husband Dan, and do the things he wanted when he was back home from his work in northern Kenya. But he'd been completely dismissive of Chloe at the finish of the marathon. She worried that there was trouble ahead in that marriage.

"There you are, my dear," cried Craig who looked refreshed after his afternoon rest. He turned towards Thabiti, who was pushing his wheelchair. "And thank you for helping me."

Thabiti looked down at handles of the wheelchair, which he began to fiddle with. "No problem." He quickly glanced up at Rose. "Marina told me to ask you if you'd like tea, or if you'd prefer something stronger?"

"I'd love a Tusker whilst I enjoy this stunning view," declared Craig.

"Some tea would be lovely," Rose said, smiling at Thabiti.

Thabiti left and Craig asked, "Would you mind moving me so I'm a little closer to the rail?"

"Of course."

Rose repositioned Craig, and as she did so, she caught a movement out of the corner of her eye. She looked up as Nina walked out of a room beyond the dining room and settled herself into a chair on a small balcony. She had her back to Rose and still wore the floppy hat with the bright red bow. Robert came out, bent over her and then returned inside.

As Rose returned to her seat, Thabiti appeared with Craig's beer. He was accompanied by a member of the lodge staff with a tray containing Rose's tea.

Robert followed them and announced, "Nina's tired and won't be joining us for supper tonight." He looked down at the tray. "Do you mind if I take her a cup of tea?"

"I can do that," said the member of staff.

Robert waved at him dismissively. "No need. I'll do it. She'd prefer not to be disturbed."

Rose pushed the tray of tea things towards Robert. "I do hope she's all right. Take these to her and tell her that if she wants any company, I'd be happy to sit with her."

"I'm sure there's no need for that," Robert answered sharply. "She just wants some tea." He picked up the tray and left.

"How very rude," commented Craig. "I'm not entirely surprised his wife wants some time to herself."

Thabiti shifted from one foot to another. "I'll go and tell Marina we are one less for supper. And I'll organise some more tea for you, Mama Rose."

Rose heard Robert say, "Here's your tea." She turned and watched him place the tray on a table on the balcony, before returning once more to his room.

CHAPTER TWENTY-THREE

It was still dark as Pearl followed her yoga companions on Sunday morning. Instead of their usual mid-morning class in the studio, Ajay had suggested an early morning session. They were walking away from the lodge to the top of the escarpment, where they could harness the dawn energy.

Pearl carried a torch in one gloved hand, a bottle of water in the other, and her yoga mat, in its protective bag, was slung over her shoulder.

Ajay whispered into the peaceful atmosphere, "Everyone find a spot, unroll your mats and face me. Be careful as we are close to the edge of the escarpment."

Pearl did as she was bid, choosing a position to the left and slightly away from the group of giggling women. Through the gloom, she spotted Wendy unrolling her mat close to Ajay.

Pearl sat down, cross-legged, to begin her meditation, and wondered about her journey to this point from a naive and frivolous girl who had only wanted to attend the most hip parties on the arm of a handsome man. But she had learnt that such men did not always respect women, and she had been used, abused and nearly killed.

She concentrated on her breathing, inhaling deeply and imagining, as she exhaled, a golden thread of breath, which carried away her worries and grievances. She felt her mind settle again and thought of blind old Mr Kariuki who had spoken to her of ancient spirits and Kikuyu history and culture.

She realised now that he had given her a feeling of belonging, and she was beginning to understand his fascination with Mount Kenya. As well as the Kikuyu belief that the creator of all things 'Ngai' descended to the mountain with the cloud, it also represented permanence and stability.

An orange glow spread across the horizon as the sun began to climb and wake the slumbering Kenyan savannah. She felt uplifted and alive.

She breathed in once more and exhaled her imaginary golden thread, expelling her deepest troubles.

She heard a sound behind her. There it was again. The noise of scuffed earth, of flattened grass, of someone walking.

Opening her eyes, she turned her head and watched the figure of a woman, with her head covered, walk slowly past and out of sight down a path at the edge of the escarpment. That was Nina Scott Watson. She recognised the large hat which obscured most of Nina's face, but why was she out so early and on her own?

Pearl shrugged. Perhaps like them she just wanted to find a place to admire the sunrise, and to be away from her domineering husband.

She turned back and could see the rest of the group more clearly. Ajay stood and said in a smooth voice, "Shall we begin?"

CHAPTER TWENTY-FOUR

R ose was surprised to hear laughter and shrill voices from the dining room as she made her way to breakfast on Sunday morning. Whilst it was usual for her to be up and about at seven thirty, she had expected the other guests to be having a lie in.

"Habari, Mama Rose," Pearl greeted her with a relaxed smile.

"Mzuri sana, habari yako?" Rose responded in Swahili.

"Mzuri,"

Rose admired the painting of the jackals, which was now hanging on the dining room wall. She presumed it was the one she had carried when she first visited the lodge with Thabiti.

"Unusual colours," commented Pearl, following her gaze.

She was right. The use of deep purple and oranges contrasted with the brown, and the artist had captured the alertness of the sitting jackal.

Rose looked around the dining room at the other members of the yoga group. She smiled as she noted that the giggling women had ignored the fresh fruit and piled their plates with a full English breakfast. The aroma of bacon made her stomach growl.

She turned back to Pearl, who was spooning muesli into a bowl, and commented, "You're all up early."

Pearl moved onto the fruit salad and replied, "Oh, this is our break. We had a wonderful early morning class on the edge of the plateau as the sun rose. I've never been one for early starts, but it was stimulating."

"I thought I might have a walk this morning," mused Rose, "And check on the jackals which the Animal Orphanage is releasing into the wild."

Pearl looked back at her, "It seems most people are inspired to be out this morning. I saw Nina in her floppy hat heading down the escarpment."

Rose drew her eyebrows together. "On her own?"

"Yes, at least I didn't see anyone else with her." Pearl picked up her bowl and sat down at the dining table.

Thabiti appeared beside Rose, and asked, "What's up? I don't like it when you have that look on your face."

Rose took his arm and led him to a corner of the dining room. "Your sister said she saw Nina walking into the conservancy on her own this morning. I'm worried. It's not safe for a girl like that to be out in Borana on her own. Anyway, what look?"

"The faraway one, which usually means you've put two and two together and don't like the answer."

Rose squeezed his shoulder. "I'm sure it's just the musing of a daft old woman. Nina will probably arrive any minute seeking a hearty breakfast after her morning walk."

They turned back to the room as Robert rushed through the doorway and cried, "Has anyone seen my wife? I can't find her."

CHAPTER TWENTY-FIVE

Marina appeared in the doorway behind Robert and cried, "I heard shouting. What's happened?"

Rose stepped forward. "It's OK. Everyone take a deep breath." She turned to Robert. "One of the other guests saw Nina out walking earlier. Do you know if she returned?"

Robert shook his head and garbled, "No. Maybe. I've no idea. When I woke up, she was gone. Why did she go for a walk? Who was with her?"

Rose placed a hand on Robert's shoulder. "She probably woke up early and went exploring. And we'll find her looking around the vegetable garden, or just sitting on a rock admiring the view."

Marina jumped in. "I'll organise the staff to search the lodge complex."

The three giggling yoga women were no longer smiling and called, "We'll help."

Marina took Robert by the arm and left the room, followed by the yoga women.

Rose caught hold of Thabiti's arm as he was about to leave, and pulled him back into the room.

She gestured to Pearl to join them and asked, "Are you certain you saw Nina this morning?"

Pearl raised her head and replied with a clear voice, "Of course. She was wearing that floppy hat of hers. You know, the one with the bright red bow."

"And what time did you see her?"

Pearl twisted her pearl earring and said, "Around half-past six. The top of the sun was just visible on the horizon. And before you ask, yes, she was alone and, no, I don't know where she was going." Pearl tugged her ear. "Actually, I'd say she was heading down the escarpment along the path we took to the watering hole where we had sundowners on Friday evening."

Rose laid a hand on Pearl's arm. "Thank you. You've been a real help, and hopefully we can find her before something dreadful happens."

Pearl responded, "I think I'll go and help with the search."

As Pearl left, Rose turned back to Thabiti. "Can you drive into the conservancy and see if you can find Nina? I think you should concentrate on the area between here and the watering hole and then widen your search from there."

Thabiti swallowed. "What about Craig? I promised to fetch him breakfast and get him dressed."

She squeezed his shoulder. "Don't worry. I'll sort that out."

Thabiti left Rose alone in the dining room. She felt she should be looking for Nina, but she couldn't abandon Craig. She poured herself a cup of tea, a coffee for Craig, and returned to their room.

"What's going on?" Craig asked the moment she entered.

"It's Nina, Robert's young wife. She's gone missing, so Marina's organising a search of the lodge grounds. And she's being assisted by the yoga group."

Rose half-lifted, half-pulled Craig into a sitting position on the bed and propped him up with her pillows. She placed his coffee on the bedside table.

"Where does Robert think she is?"

"He has no idea. But Pearl saw her out walking this morning, and she was on her own." Rose walked over to the large window and stared out. "Craig, I'm worried. A young naive girl like that. Somewhere out there." She gestured with her arm across the window. "Anything could happen to her."

There was a knock on the door. Rose opened it to find an agitated Marina, who couldn't stand still, and a concerned-looking Julius.

"There's no sign of her," Marina gabbled. "I don't know what to do."

Rose placed her arms on Marina's shoulders and pushed down. "Breathe. And stop panicking."

Marina stilled but continued to wring her hands.

Rose continued, "I asked Thabiti to drive into the conservancy and look for Nina there. Pearl is certain she saw her walking down the escarpment and thinks she was heading towards the watering hole. You know, the one where we had sundowners. Nina probably wanted to watch the early morning wildlife."

Julius raised his hand and said, "Mama Rose. That's what I came to tell you. I've been out at the jackal pen all night. I opened the gate so the jackals could wander into the conservancy, but I still wanted to keep a watch on them."

"And did they go out?"

He bobbed his head from side to side. "Two did and two didn't. I've shut the enclosure gate now but I'll go back tonight, open it and keep watch."

Marina interjected, "But what has this to do with the missing Nina?"

"Well, I saw someone walking through the bush towards the watering hole. I think it was a mzungu but couldn't be clear as something was covering their head. Anyway, about twenty minutes later I heard the sound of a car engine."

Marina clapped her hand to her mouth. "Oh no. She's been kidnapped. We need to find her. Come on Mama Rose, I'll drive."

Rose hesitated and looked back into the bedroom where she met Craig's concerned gaze. "I can't leave Craig on his own."

"But we need to find Nina."

Julius coughed. "Perhaps I could keep Bwana Hardie company and fetch him whatever he needs."

"But you've been up all night," Rose said. "And you need some sleep."

Marina gasped. "But not until you've eaten. You must be hungry. Why don't you go to the dining room, collect breakfast for yourself and Craig, and eat with him in his room?" She looked through Rose's open bedroom door.

"That's very kind of you. And I am hungry. Don't worry, Mama Rose, I will look after Bwana Hardie."

"Sorted," cried Marina.

Rose's mouth was dry as Julius entered the room and she spotted his red-rimmed eyes.

She turned to Craig.

He nodded at her. "I'll be fine. Go and help Marina before she turns herself inside out with worry."

Rose closed the door and followed Marina. At the end of the corridor she turned and looked back, and felt a chill in her bones.

CHAPTER TWENTY-SIX

R ose knew her own driving could be erratic when she was in a hurry, but that was nothing compared with Marina. She was jolted forward as the car hit a hole and was relieved to be wearing her seat belt.

"Marina, please slow down. We can't look for Nina or any evidence of her at this pace. And I'd prefer not to arrive at the watering hole battered and bruised."

The car slowed and Marina drove around a lyceum bush rather than over it and called, "Sorry."

"Thank you," Rose sighed.

She looked around the deserted landscape, but when she caught a movement in the corner of her eye, she realised it wasn't empty. She spotted a herd of impala and nearby, three zebra were grazing quietly.

They reached the watering hole and Marina parked the car. The empty sundowners platform was to their left and a thicket of large whistling thorn bushes to their right.

She heard an engine and Thabiti appeared in another of the lodge's long wheelbase safari Land Cruisers.

They all walked to the sundowner's platform. A huge lone bull elephant was squirting water over its back as it stood at the edge of the watering hole.

Thabiti twirled his car keys. "There's no sign of her, but I can't look in every nook and cranny. Borana's huge."

Rose watched the elephant. "This is an obvious place for her to have walked to, especially as she was here on Friday night. And both Pearl and Julius thought they saw her walking in this direction."

Rose turned around and faced Marina and Thabiti. "Let's have a good look for her. I suggest we walk the perimeter of the watering hole and search any obvious hiding places, and near any rocks or mounds which she might have fallen off."

They left the platform and walked towards the thicket of whistling thorn bushes. Thabiti walked with his hands in his pockets and Marina was unusually quiet. Marina pushed through the bushes, but the thorns on a branch caught the back of her t-shirt.

"Just a minute," said Rose as she carefully pulled the spikes and the branch free. She followed Marina and was surprised to find a clearing inside the thicket.

"Look," cried Marina, as she rushed forward. She scrabbled by a clump of sedges with long grass-like fronds, and pulled out a floppy hat with a bright red bow. She patted it down to remove the dust. "So Nina has been taken."

"And look at this." Thabiti was squatting down at the other side of the clearing where some of the sedges had been flattened. "The ground is boggy and there look to be tyre marks, as if a car has been parked here."

Rose felt the hairs rise on the back of her neck. She looked around sharply and although she didn't see anyone, her feeling of unease remained.

Marina picked at the hat's red bow. "What are we going to do? We can't just lose a guest."

Rose tried not to think the worst. "I know, but just because it looks like a car was parked here, it doesn't mean she's been kidnapped. The car may have had nothing to do with her disappearance, or whoever it was might have offered to drive her around the conservancy.

"Look, she may have been injured and been taken to another lodge or the nearest hospital. There are plenty of explanations."

Marina stretched up her hands and took a deep breath. "Of course, you're right, Mama Rose. I'm so grateful you're here to consider this logically. We should get back to the lodge and then I can radio the other lodges, security and the conservancy management team to find out if they've seen Nina. And after that I'll call the local hospitals in Isiolo and Nanyuki."

"That's a good idea." Rose rubbed her chin. "But I also think we should inform someone in a position of responsibility."

Marina's eyes gleamed as she exclaimed, "Sam. We must tell Sam. I saw him after the marathon yesterday and he told me he and Judy were staying in the tented camp at Lewa last night. Oh, I do hope he hasn't left. He might know what to do."

Thabiti stood up, but still studied the wet ground. "By Judy, do you mean Constable Wachira?"

"Oh yes, of course," responded Marina.

"That's exactly who we need to find," agreed Rose. She addressed Thabiti, "Can you drive across to Lewa and see if they're still there?"

Turning back to Marina, she said, "And I think we'll have to go back and update Robert. He's not going to like our news."

CHAPTER TWENTY-SEVEN

As Marina parked the car at the back of Aureus Lodge, Julius rushed out of the main building. He was red in the face and flapping his hands.

Rose's mouth tasted sour as she flung open the door. "What's the matter? Has Nina been found? Is she hurt?"

Julius's voice was shaky as he replied, "It's Bwana Hardie. Pole, Mama. It's all my fault. I must have fallen asleep after eating such a wonderful breakfast. And he must have tried to get up. And then he fell."

Rose felt a lump rise in her throat and she rushed past Julius into the lodge.

Her legs gave way when she saw Craig lying on the bed. She flopped down beside him. She gently stroked his clammy forehead and looked into his pale face.

"What …" Her voice caught in her throat, so she swallowed and tried again. "What happened? Are you hurt?"

"I'm sorry to be so much trouble," Craig croaked. "I really needed the bathroom."

"And Julius had fallen asleep?"

"Yes, I'm sorry." He shifted his weight to look at her and cried out, "Ow."

She shook herself. She needed to get up and check Craig. To see if he was injured. To see if he needed to go to hospital.

She took a deep breath and said softly but firmly, "Please try to stay still, and tell me, where did it hurt just then?"

"It's my hip," Craig grunted. "My left one. I'm used to it hurting, but it's worse now. There's like a stabbing pain."

She shuffled off the bed and leaned over him. Carefully, she pulled down the top of his pyjama trousers, revealing a bruised and swollen hip. She gently examined it.

"Ow," Craig cried out again.

"Oh dear, you may have fractured it, which is a common injury when people our age fall. I'm so sorry, but there's not much I can do. You need to go to hospital to have it examined."

He grasped her arm and pleaded, "Not Nairobi. Don't airlift me there. Can you give me some painkillers and drive me to Nanyuki? To the Cottage Hospital?"

Rose clenched her jaw. "Are you worried about the expense? About the cost of the Nairobi hospital?"

Craig screwed his eyes in pain. "It's not just that. I don't want to be all the way down in Nairobi when you are up in Nanyuki. And I want to see Chris and be close to our friends."

She found a blanket and laid it over him. "OK. Let me try to contact Dr Farrukh and see what she says. I do hope she's taking calls today, as it is Sunday. And she can also recommend what painkillers to give you. I'm not sure what procedure you'll have when you arrive at the hospital, but they'll probably start by X-raying your hip."

There was a tap on the open door and Marina called, "Can I come in?"

"Yes, do," said Rose as she walked across to the doorway.

Marina handed her a cup of tea. "I thought you might like this."

Rose took the cup gratefully and sipped the sweetened liquid.

"I hope it's OK?" whispered Marina. "I added some sugar."

Rose placed her free arm on Marina's. "Thank you, my dear. It's just what I need."

"How is he?"

"I'm alive," declared Craig, "And there's no need to whisper. Ow."

Rose carried her tea back to Craig's bedside and squeezed his hand with her free one. Looking at Marina she said, "He's in quite a lot of pain. I think he's fractured his hip, so I need to contact the Cottage Hospital."

Marina tugged at her hair, and said, "You'd better call from my office, as it has the best reception. I can show you where it is, but will Craig be all right on his own?"

Julius's bowed head appeared around the door. He wore a clean green uniform and was wringing his hat in his hands.

"I would like to make amends for my earlier mistake. Please let me stay with Bwana Hardie."

Rose examined Julius, who was alert and showed no signs of his earlier fatigue. "Thank you," she replied, and followed Marina to the lodge office.

Marina picked up a mobile phone and said, "I just called the Cottage Hospital about Nina, but they haven't admitted any mzungu women today."

She pressed some keys on the phone and handed it to Rose. She whispered, "I'll be in the kitchen. It's just over there." She pointed to a single-storey building with higher walls and less thatching than its neighbours.

Rose nodded as a voice answered her call. "Habari, Cottage Hospital. How can I help you?"

"Oh, hello. Can I speak with Dr Farrukh?" she asked.

"Which one? Dr Jasmine Farrukh is on duty this morning?" The efficient female voice responded.

Rose felt her body sag in relief. "Oh good, that's exactly who I want to speak to. This is Rose Hardie. My husband, Craig, has had a fall at a lodge in Borana, and I think he's injured his hip. I'm going to drive him to you, but I wanted to let Dr Farrukh know he's coming, and ask her what painkillers I can give him."

The voice answered, "Just a minute. I'll patch you through."

The line was silent for several minutes and then Rose heard Dr Farrukh's calm voice asking, "Is that Rose?"

"Yes, my apologies for disturbing you on a Sunday, but Craig's had a fall. And I think he's fractured his hip."

"I understand you are in Borana? Can you get him here?"

"Yes, I'll drive him to you. But it may take a couple of hours and he's in pain. What shall I give him?"

"He can have some paracetamol, but definitely no ibuprofen. I'm going off duty shortly, but phone the hospital when you reach Timau and they can call me back in."

"Oh, thank you. I'm really grateful," sighed Rose.

"No problem," said Dr Farrukh. "Now I must complete my rounds. I'll see you later, but call the hospital number if you have any problems. As you know, we do have an ambulance, but it's old and Craig will have a much smoother ride in your car."

Rose finished the call with relief, but she still felt a fluttering in her stomach. Now she had to try to find the most comfortable way to transport

Craig. Probably by reclining the front seat of the Subaru.

The hardest part would be getting him in and out. And the road through the Ngare Ndare forest was so damaged and full of potholes.

Marina broke into her thoughts as she asked, "Are you OK?"

Rose shook her head to clear it and answered, "The Cottage Hospital are expecting us. I was just trying to work out the route. Going through the Ngare Ndare is quickest, but I'm worried that the journey will be too arduous."

"Why not go through Lewa and out onto the Isiolo road?" suggested Marina. "As you know, that road is tarmacked all the way to Nanyuki. So although it might be longer, it's probably quicker as you would have to go really slowly though the forest. Do you need someone to come with you?"

Rose hesitated. It would be reassuring to have a companion just in case something happened, or Craig's condition worsened. But what about Nina? She was still missing and needed to be found.

She replied, "I'm sure we'll be all right. You're busy here with your guests and now Nina is missing. Your hands are full. Is there any news?"

Marina's shoulders slumped. "My call to the Cottage Hospital was the last one. None of the other hospitals have admitted her and there's been no sighting of her on Borana or at any of the lodges here or on Lewa."

Marina's voice increased in pitch as she cried, "It's as if she's vanished into thin air."

They walked past the kitchen. The aroma of roast lamb wafted out of the open window and Rose's stomach gurgled.

Marina exclaimed, "You didn't have any breakfast." She stopped and patted Rose's arm. "Wait here, I'll just organise something for you to take back with you, and a sandwich for the journey."

As Marina stepped into the kitchen, Pearl appeared from the main lodge building and asked, "Have you seen Thabiti? I was hoping he might give me a lift home."

"He's gone to Lewa, to tell the authorities that Nina's missing," Rose replied.

Pearl lowered her head. "Never mind. The others are all staying until tomorrow, but I was hoping to get back to Nanyuki." She turned back towards the lodge.

Rose started. "Just a minute," she called. "I could give you a lift and it would really help me out. I'm taking Craig to the Cottage Hospital and I'd love some company on the journey, just in case something happens. It'll be slow, though, as I'm driving out through Lewa."

"Ok, thanks. I'll just go and pack. Are you leaving soon?" Pearl asked.

"Just as soon as I get organised and get Craig into the car," replied Rose.

CHAPTER TWENTY-EIGHT

Thabiti drove east towards Lewa Conservancy. As he looked around, he felt alone and slightly afraid. Growing up, he'd spent most of his time in Kenya's bustling capital city, Nairobi, with only the occasional trip to a safari lodge.

And there had always been other people in charge. Other people to rely on.

He steadied the car as the black-soil road turned a corner into a hidden dip. He always thought of the savannah as vast open plains which were predominantly flat, but Borana was not like that.

There were many rocky outcrops, numerous low hills, and small, concealed dells.

The landscape often appeared empty as the changing terrain seemed to break up the view and camouflage the wildlife. Here, animals tended to be in smaller groups, often hidden in the contours of the lands. But then he'd have a surprise, like now.

He slowed the car again and steadily passed a black rhino wrapping its mouth around the branch of a white thorn acacia bush. It seemed quite content being by itself in this vast landscape.

But what about Nina, all alone out here? What had made her wander off into the conservancy? If she'd wanted to visit the watering hole, to watch the animals in the early morning, why hadn't she asked for a guide?

He guessed this is what people referred to as the English reserve, and that she was more afraid of asking for someone's help, than walking by herself in a dangerous wildlife area.

A discrete sign told him he was passing into Lewa Conservancy and two miles further on he spotted some of the marathon tents. There were fewer of them, and the starting line had been dismantled, but people were wandering around and there was a cluster of tables and chairs by a catering tent.

He parked next to the tent and recognised the catering company as the Rusty Nail, who had served food at the Rhino Charge at the beginning of May. His first experience of that event was not one he cared to remember.

"Thabiti," a voice shouted. "Is Marina not feeding you?"

He looked around in confusion and spotted Sam, sitting with Judy, several tables away. He joined them and his stomach grumbled as he smelt their partially eaten egg and bacon breakfast rolls. "Habari. Actually, I haven't had a chance to eat breakfast yet."

Sam leaned forward. "If you've sacrificed your breakfast, it means that something important has happened or there's trouble. Which is it?"

Thabiti looked down and played with the thousand bob note he'd found in his pocket. "Trouble. But I'm starving. Can I get some breakfast and then tell you?" He looked up at Sam and then away at the Rusty Nail Catering tent. There was no queue.

"Off you go," said Sam. "I know you think better with something in your stomach."

Thabiti returned to the table with a breakfast roll and a Stoney Tangawizi ginger beer. He took a grateful bite out of his roll.

"So," said Sam. "Mama Rose is staying at the lodge and there is trouble. What a surprise." He tapped a finger on the table.

Thabiti swallowed and responded, "It's nothing to do with Mama Rose. You see, we've an English couple staying with us, friends of the owners. Well actually, I'm not sure they are friends."

Thabiti picked at the label on his bottle of Tangawizi. "Anyway, the owners offered them the use of the lodge over the marathon weekend. The husband, Robert, I don't like him. He's rude and ... pretentious. But his wife is sweet. She's called Nina, and I think she's quite a bit younger than he is.

"Anyway, they both ran in the half marathon yesterday and Nina was tired so she didn't join us for supper. But."

Thabiti stopped and took a swig of his ginger beer.

Judy, who'd been silent up to now, leaned forward and asked, "Has something happened to this Nina?"

Thabiti swallowed and nodded. He looked at her and then back at his bottle. "She's missing. Pearl saw her out walking this morning, but she didn't return."

"I presume you've looked all around the lodge," the young constable probed.

Thabiti looked up. "It was the first thing Marina did. She organised a group of staff and guests to search all over the lodge and the grounds."

Sam sat up and crossed his arms, and his jaw was set into a serious expression. "But there was no sign of the English woman."

Thabiti looked around the camp and back at the table. "No. Mama Rose suggested I drive into the conservancy and look for her there, but it's far too big for me to search properly, particularly with all the hills and hidden hollows. Anyway, I didn't find her, either."

"And there was no other sign of her?" Judy picked up a white paper cup and drank her tea.

"Julius said he saw someone in the conservancy, close to his jackal pen. And a little later the sound of a car engine."

"Who is Julius?" Judy asked.

"Oh, he's the head warden at the Mount Kenya Animal Orphanage. He and Mama Rose are releasing some young jackals back into the wild. Anyway, he told Mama Rose what he'd seen, so she and Marina started their own search of the conservancy."

Thabiti rubbed the back of his neck. "I met them at a watering hole where we'd previously had sundowners and next to it, in a clearing in some whistling thorn trees, we found Nina's hat. And I found what looked like a tyre mark in the wet ground."

Thabiti took another gulp of his Tangawizi. He leaned back and felt the blood rush to his face. He wasn't used to making such long speeches.

Sam placed both of his arms on the table and leaned forward. "So you think someone either took Nina or she'd arranged to meet someone there. Either way, she's disappeared."

Judy looked from Thabiti to Sam and said, "Just because you found her hat in a clearing with a tyre mark, it doesn't mean she left in the car. She could still be out in the conservancy."

"Dead or alive," conceded Sam in a sombre tone.

CHAPTER TWENTY-NINE

Rose drove Craig's Subaru steadily along the black-soil track into Lewa Conservancy. Through the driver's mirror, she saw Pearl gazing out at the landscape.

"Oh," moaned Craig beside her. She laid her hand on his arm. As she'd expected, manoeuvring him into the front seat of the car had been difficult for her and the lodge staff, and painful for Craig.

Still, he was in now and she was driving him back to Nanyuki, and the Cottage Hospital where he'd be able to get help.

She drove through the marathon area which was much quieter than the previous day. People wandered around or stood in groups chatting. As she slowed down, she spotted Sam's sizeable figure, sitting at a table with Thabiti and Constable Wachira, or Judy, as she liked to be called.

She parked, looked across at Craig and asked, "Are you OK for a few minutes? I just want to speak to Thabiti, Sam and Constable Wachira."

"I'll be fine," Craig groaned. "I'll just have a rest." He closed his eyes.

"Have you seen Thabiti?" Pearl asked from the back.

Rose and Pearl climbed out of the car. Pearl approached Thabiti whilst Rose greeted Sam and Constable Wachira. She just couldn't get the hang of calling her Judy.

"Habari, Mama Rose," said Sam in a guarded tone. "Have you brought more news of the missing English woman?"

"Nina? I'm afraid there was still no sign of her when I left the lodge. Marina's called round the hospitals and lodges, but nobody's seen her. No. I'm driving Craig to Nanyuki. He's had a fall and needs treatment at the Cottage Hospital."

Constable Wachira placed a hand gently on her arm. "I'm sorry to hear that. Are you all right driving him?"

Rose turned to her. "Thank you. Pearl, Thabiti's sister, is with us as I'm giving her a lift home."

Thabiti and Pearl joined them. The taller Pearl locked eyes with the athletic constable until the latter said in a respectful tone, "It's good to meet you."

"And you," replied Pearl in a matching tone.

Thabiti kicked a small stone on the ground and said, "I'm so sorry to hear about Craig. Will he be all right?"

Rose rubbed her chin. "Do you know, I'm not so sure he will be. It's the pain. There's only so much he can take, and this injury, on top of the pain and damage from the polio and its secondary disease, well ..." She felt her eyes sting with tears.

The group was silent.

She wiped her eyes and said, "But you must continue to look for Nina. I'm not sure if she went off in a car or is still somewhere out in the wild." She turned to Sam and asked, "What do you suggest we do?"

"If Judy doesn't mind," he turned to Constable Wachira, who nodded in acceptance, "I think we should follow Thabiti back to the lodge. We can question the other guests and conduct our own search. It might be worthwhile calling in Reuben and the Lewa tracker dogs, that's if we still think she might be out in the conservancy."

Constable Wachira added, "But I'm not sure we'll get all that done today and return to Nanyuki tonight."

Pearl added in a casual voice, "So why don't you stay at the lodge? There's plenty of space. You can use my room, which was set apart from the others."

Thabiti looked up at Pearl and then at Sam. "That's a great idea. And as Mama Rose is leaving, it would be a relief to have someone to head the investigation."

CHAPTER THIRTY

Rose drove through the centre of Nanyuki, which seemed to be sleeping through the remainder of Sunday morning. She knew many of the inhabitants would be at church with one of the numerous and varied religious denominations who held services on Sunday mornings.

She took a left turn and continued along a track towards the Cottage Hospital. A plume of dust followed her as she drove past the entrance to Podo School, and opposite it, Tony the woodman's locked workshop. Pieces of wood and various works-in-progress were scattered around the building.

She slowed down, not wanting to cover the lone figure walking in front of her with dust. As she passed the pedestrian, she realised it was Chris, and she immediately braked to a stop and wound down the car window.

Chris squatted by the car and said, "Hi, are you coming for lunch at Cape …" He looked across at his father and stopped. For a moment he appeared shocked into silence and then he asked in a serious tone, "What's the matter? What happened?"

Rose answered as calmly as she could, "He's had a fall, back at the lodge. So I'm taking him to the Cottage Hospital, and Dr Farrukh's meeting us so she can evaluate him."

Chris's head disappeared as he stood up.

Rose waited, uncertain what to do next.

Chris bent down again and spoke through the open window. "I'll meet you at the hospital entrance."

He jogged away in front. Slowly and stiffly at first but, as Rose followed, he loosened up and ran with a relaxed stride. Rose passed him as she drove onto the gravelled hospital entrance road.

Rose sat beside Craig's bed in a small ward in the Cottage Hospital. The two beds opposite Craig's were occupied by African men, and the one beside him was empty.

She stroked his arm, which lay on top of the crisp white sheet, and asked, "How do you feel now?"

His voice was weak as he answered, "Like I ran in yesterday's marathon, but alongside a herd of buffalo. The pain's a dull ache now, not the stabbing it was. But I feel rather drowsy."

"I know," Rose said. "You need to rest, but can you hold on until the doctor arrives?"

"I'll try." Craig gave her a fragile smile.

"What's wrong with him?" asked a voice from the other side of the room.

She stood and walked across to the bed where the speaker lay. He was an elderly African man.

"That's my husband, Craig," Rose told him. "He fell and injured his hip. What about you?"

"I went to church, tripped over a chair and sprained my ankle. And he," his eyes moved in the direction of the bed next to him, "fell off his boda boda."

Dr Farrukh bustled into the room, followed by Chris, and they gathered around Craig's bed.

The doctor placed two X-ray negatives on top of the sheets.

She looked at Craig and said, "You were lucky. There is a small fracture in the upper portion of the femur, but it has not extended all the way across."

Rose looked at the X-rays, but without her glasses it was hard to see where the damage was.

Chris asked, "Can you show me where that is?"

"Here," Dr Farrukh indicated with the tip of her pen. "The crack is at the top of the femoral neck, just below the ball of the ball-and-socket joint."

"What does it mean?" asked Rose.

Dr Farrukh straightened up and looked across at her. "I'm afraid surgery is not an option. There's too much risk at Craig's age, particularly with his recent medical history."

"No operation," Craig croaked.

Rose moved to the top of the bed and stroked his thinning hair. "I know, no surgery."

The doctor continued, "As he's not very mobile, which is both an advantage and a disadvantage, he's unlikely to cause any further damage, as long as he promises not to try to move by himself again." The doctor's eyes narrowed as she looked down at Craig, and then her expression softened.

She turned back to Rose and said in an apologetic tone, "Unfortunately, his lack of weight-bearing movement will reduce the rate at which his hip heals. And of course, this is the side that has been damaged by his polio, which might inhibit the process."

Rose clasped her hands in front of her. "So what do you suggest we do?"

"I'd like to keep him under observation for a few days. And reduce any unnecessary movement. We can monitor his blood pressure and his painkillers. Also, I'm concerned that there may be additional damage to the blood vessels to the ball-and-socket joint, which we need to monitor."

Rose's mouth was dry as she asked in a choked voice, "He will be able to come home, won't he?"

Dr Farrukh looked at her with sadness in her eyes. "I'm not sure. But I hope so. Let's take each day one at a time."

She moved around the bed, squeezed Rose's shoulder and added, "If you don't mind, I have to return home. Work is always so busy, with my husband and I both being doctors here, so we try to have a family meal on Sundays."

The doctor left and Rose stroked Craig's head again. He looked peaceful and she realised he was sleeping. She hoped it was pain free.

"Is he asleep?" Chris whispered.

She nodded.

"So what are you going to do?"

She looked around the small room and answered in a quiet, unsure voice, "I don't know."

Chris wrapped his arm around her and led her out into the corridor. "I bet you haven't eaten today."

She felt in a daze, and the sights and the sounds of the hospital dulled around her. She responded weakly, "Marina packed me some food from the lodge. I suppose I'll go home and eat that."

Chris stopped, stood opposite her and held her by both her arms.

She felt him peering at her as he said, "I don't think it's a good idea, being on your own at the moment. And you need to eat, as you have to keep your strength up. You know it's going to be a difficult week. Come on, we'll go to Cape Chestnut for Sunday lunch. That's where I was heading when we met."

They walked down the concrete steps at the front of the hospital to the parked Subaru.

Automatically, she removed the keys from her pocket, but then stood still, wondering what to do next.

Chris took the keys and said gently but firmly, "I think I'll drive."

CHAPTER THIRTY-ONE

Cape Chestnut was buzzing with diners who were either eating and drinking, or waiting for the queue to reduce so they could approach the Sunday lunch buffet.

Chris led Rose between occupied tables and whilst she felt some people speak to her, she couldn't understand what they were saying.

Chris pulled out a chair, and she sat down at a small wooden table under the shade of the large Cape chestnut tree, after which the restaurant was named. She looked up and felt its strength and permanency.

Suddenly, she found the noise from the restaurant deafening, and she covered her ears to block it out. Chris mouthed something at her. Slowly, she removed her hands, and whilst there was a lot of chatter, some laughter and a sudden shout, the noise was now bearable.

"Will you be all right for a few minutes while I go to the bar?"

Chris walked towards the single-story wooden restaurant building with its outdoor, covered veranda on which the buffet was set up. Rose remembered that this had been one of the original colonial houses in Nanyuki.

Before becoming a restaurant, it had been used by some local mums when they set up Podo School. The school had flourished as more people moved to Nanyuki, including British army families, and purpose-built classrooms had been constructed on the larger adjacent site.

She could still hear the cries of children, and looked around the garden. Three young boys and a girl were playing in a sandpit, overseen by two grim-faced African ayahs.

Chris returned, placed a glass of amber coloured liquid in front of her and announced, "Brandy. Purely medicinal, of course."

Gingerly, she took a sip. It was sweet and fruity and warmed her throat. She took another, longer drink and the liquid began to warm her insides and clear the fog in her brain.

"Why don't I get us both lunch?" Chris suggested. "Do you want curry or Sunday roast?"

She looked at him and blinked. "Um, I think the roast."

She was on her own again. As she looked around, several people raised a hand or shouted a greeting to her. She began to raise her hand in response, but returned it to the table. She stared at her half-empty glass.

Was this the end for Craig? She thought she had been preparing for it, but whilst she had said the right words, she realised she hadn't actually believed them. Because she didn't want to. Chris was in Kenya now, but he would soon return to his own life, and Heather was happily settled in the UK.

She looked around again at all the merry faces. She knew many of them had their own struggles and she had lent a hand, or listened to the troubles of one or another of them on numerous occasions.

Without many of the distractions of the modern world, they were a tight-knit community, and she knew she could rely on them to help her when Craig passed. Feeling some reassurance, she took another sip of brandy and felt her shoulders loosen as some of the tension left them.

Chris placed a white plate in front of her containing modest portions of roast chicken and lamb, roast potatoes and salad. Automatically, she lifted her knife and fork and began to eat. She was hungry. For several minutes, they ate in contented silence.

Chris laid down his knife and fork, leant back and drank his Tusker beer. He asked, "Is there anything that needs doing at your cottage before Dad returns? At least it's single storey so you don't need to worry about stairs, or creating a downstairs bedroom. But what about the bathroom?"

Rose looked up at Chris. "Your Dad hasn't been able to bathe on his own for some time. In fact, he hasn't been able to move around or dress himself for several weeks now. Samwell is an unexpected star and has been helping me, and Kipto. I don't think there is anything we can do, but pray he is well enough to return home."

Chris leaned forward and took hold of her hand. "I hadn't realised he'd deteriorated so much. Your emails were so upbeat and full of news of the people and places you and Dad were visiting. I know he had a mini-stroke when I was last here, but I thought he had recovered.

"Many people do. That's why I wasn't in a rush to return. I didn't know. I didn't realise." Chris paused. "Dad's dying, isn't he?"

She wiped a tear from the corner of her eye and replied, "Yes, he is, but I can't accept it. Not yet."

CHAPTER THIRTY-TWO

R ose finished most of her main course. A waiter cleared her plate away and replaced it with a glass of chocolate mousse. She looked up as another figure approached their table.

"Hi Rose, Chris," said Chloe, as she nodded towards Chris. "Do you mind if I join you?"

"Is the major here?" asked Chris.

"Yes, Dan is with his BATUK mates." Chloe indicated with her hand but did not look back at the tables full of noisy diners.

Chris pushed his chair back, stood and offered it to Chloe as he said, "Here, have my seat. I'll go and join them for a short time. Is that OK, Mum?" He looked down at Rose.

She smiled weakly. "Of course. Thank you for getting me lunch and sitting with me."

Chris squeezed her shoulder, then left.

Chloe sat down and looked across at Rose with her eyebrows drawn together. "Is something wrong? You look rather pale. And I thought you and Craig were staying at the lodge with Marina and Thabiti until tomorrow." Her hand flew to her mouth. "Is it Craig? Where is he?"

Rose placed both arms on the table in front of her and leaned forward. She said in a hoarse voice, "Craig had an accident at the lodge. A fall. So I brought him back to the Cottage Hospital."

She sat up, sipped her brandy wine and continued in a stronger tone. "He's damaged his hip, which is common after a fall, but it's his left hip, the one that's damaged by polio. And because he's no longer mobile, Dr Farrukh is worried that it might not heal."

Chloe leaned forward and placed her hand on Rose's arm. "I'm so sorry. How long do they expect to keep him in hospital?"

Rose looked down at her uneaten dessert. "They're not sure. Not sure if he will ever come home." She rubbed her forehead and covered her eyes with her free hand.

"Maybe he just needs some time. Who knows, in a couple of days his condition could improve and he could be ready to leave hospital," Chloe said as she removed her sunglasses.

Rose sniffed and looked at Chloe. "I do hope so." She noticed that Chloe's eyes were bloodshot and her face was puffy. "But I'm not the only one with problems, am I?"

Chloe replaced her sunglasses and leaned back in her chair. "I don't know what else to do. I've tried so hard, doing the things Dan wants to do, like coming here for lunch with all his BATUK mates, but does he appreciate it? No, and he forgets I'm there half the time. But if I want to do my own thing he gets annoyed. I can't seem to win."

"And you've tried talking to him, and telling him how you feel?"

"Of course. But he barely listens and drones on about how tough his job is, and how hard it is being away from home so much. And just now I could really do with some support." Chloe removed a tissue from her small shoulder bag, turned away from Rose and blew her nose.

Chloe continued, "Sorry, you have your own worries and problems to deal with."

Rose replied, "I've always got time to help you. And it's good for me to remember that other people have their own problems. Besides, it stops me dwelling on what might or might not happen. Tell me about it."

Chloe turned back to Rose and once again removed her sunglasses and secured them in her long blonde hair. She leant forward and spoke slowly and quietly.

"I've been seeing a counsellor. Actually, the one you recommended. And she's really helped me come to terms with my miscarriages and my inability to keep a baby. It's the reason I was running for the Baby Loss Awareness charity at

Lewa. It's all part of coming to terms with the issue and the beginning of my healing process. But I'm not even sure Dan is aware I'm attending the sessions."

"Have you told him? Or talked through anything the counsellor has said?" Rose asked.

Chloe twisted her wedding ring. "No, the time never seems to be quite right. But he's only home for a few more days and then who knows how long he'll be away for."

Rose leant towards Chloe. "You really need to try to get him to understand before he leaves. Would he attend a counselling session with you?"

Chloe scoffed. "I doubt it. You know what the army boys are like about not admitting to any weakness, never mind their own feelings."

"Then you really need to approach it from the angle of helping you. Something along the lines of, 'you're really going to miss him when he's away and that you are also finding life hard when you're on your own, particularly as you keep worrying about not being able to have a baby.

"And would he mind providing moral support at one of your counselling sessions?' Something like that. Make it seem that the issue is all with you and that he is being a chivalrous husband by accompanying you."

"OK, I'll try." Chloe eyed Rose's chocolate mousse. "Are you going to eat that?"

Rose pushed the dessert towards Chloe.

"I shouldn't," Chloe said as she picked up a spoon, "but I feel like comfort eating."

Rose smiled. "And you did run a marathon yesterday. That was a real achievement. Do you feel stiff this morning?"

Chloe waved the spoon in the air. "A little. But we met more of Dan's mates at Kongoni's this morning, so I went for a swim, which I think helped. Another English lady arrived and joined me. She'd also run in the marathon yesterday."

Chloe ate another spoonful of mousse and then pushed the half-eaten dessert away. "So how is Aureus Lodge? I'm sure Marina is being her usual efficient self, but what about Thabiti? How is he coping with the guests?"

"They're both doing admirably, particularly in the difficult circumstances." Rose looked up into the branches of the Cape chestnut tree.

"What circumstances?"

"One of the guests, an English woman, has gone missing. It appears she walked off into Borana Conservancy on her own this morning and hasn't been seen since. I do hope she returns to the lodge before nightfall."

CHAPTER THIRTY-THREE

On Sunday evening, Thabiti sat with Judy and Sam on the wooden viewing deck outside the drawing room of Aureus Lodge. Marina had taken the yoga group on their final game drive before they departed the following morning.

Sam, and Judy, in her official police role as Constable Wachira, had spent most of the afternoon questioning the members of the yoga retreat and Robert Scott Watson about Nina's disappearance.

Thabiti placed a diet coke for Judy, and Tusker beers for himself and Sam, on a small wooden coffee table and sat down in a wooden framed safari chair with a canvas seat. He opened his beer and without looking up asked hesitantly, "Did you find out anything else about Nina's disappearance?"

Sam opened his beer and took a long drink. "Very little," he replied and wiped his mouth with the back of his hand.

Judy removed a small notebook from her trouser pocket, which she opened. Reading the pages, she commented, "The members of the yoga retreat were at a dawn class on the edge of the escarpment, but, unlike your sister, none of them remembers seeing Nina, or anyone else for that matter. Apparently they were all centring themselves and becoming one with nature as the sun rose."

Sam added, "And none of them had met Nina before this weekend, or so they say."

Thabiti flicked the ring pull on his can. "I took a gin and tonic to Robert in his room earlier, but he only grunted at me."

Sam sat back and crossed his arms over his chest. "He's a difficult one to read. He's certainly worried, but in his shoes I would be desperate to be out there." He indicated towards the conservancy. "Looking for my wife. But instead, he's sitting in his room fretting about her disappearance, and snapping at anyone who approaches him."

Thabiti looked up at Sam and then over his shoulder towards Robert's room, beyond the dining room.

The door onto the small balcony was open, so he whispered, "You know, I don't like Robert that much. And he's not very loving towards Nina, considering they're on their honeymoon. So I'm not surprised she wanted to walk out. I would leave him, too. But not here. Not in the middle of Borana."

Judy consulted her notebook again. "Her husband said she didn't know anyone in Kenya, and that it was his idea to spend their honeymoon here and take part in the Lewa Marathon."

Sam stood, leaned against the platform rail and stared into the conservancy as the light dimmed.

He said, "There are two sets of headlights returning to the lodge. Presumably Marina and the car you sent out to search for Nina?"

Thabiti stared down at a shortwave radio on the table. "As neither of them radioed in, I doubt they've found her."

Judy shivered and said, "Poor girl, out there on her own. She must be terrified."

Sam collected a shuka blanket from a small pile by the entrance to the drawing room, unfolded it, and draped it over Judy's shoulders. "I've spoken to Reuben at Lewa Conservancy," he said.

"If Nina hasn't returned by the morning, he'll bring the tracker dogs over to search for her. They might have more luck than us."

They all drank in silence for a few minutes.

Thabiti looked across at Judy and said, "Well done in the marathon yesterday. You make me feel rather inadequate, only doing the half, and Marina and I walked much of the way."

"Thank you. But I've been training, whereas I understand you took someone's entry at the last minute."

Thabiti looked into the drawing room and answered, "Yes, the owners of this lodge. The wife was injured, so they didn't come over from the UK. They offered their marathon places to Marina and me, and the use of the lodge to the Scott Watsons." He looked back at Sam and asked, "Have you ever taken part?"

"Oh, yes, back in the day, when I was my younger, fitter self." Sam clasped his hands together. "But now I'm happy supporting those who are competing, and I enjoy organising the timing equipment."

Thabiti leaned forward and said, "So you use transponder chips in the competitors' numbers to track their times? Is there monitoring equipment along the route or just at the start and finish?"

Sam tapped his thumbs together. "At the start the equipment just confirms the numbers who cross the starting line. The time begins for all the runners when the starter shouts 'go'."

Thabiti bit his lip and picked up his beer can. "So the time I was given was not my true 'running time' as it took us several minutes to get through the start."

"Yes, that's right. It's why they call the elite runners forward to the front, so they can be through the start and away for a true race, and the fun runners follow."

There was a crackle on the radio. Gingerly, Thabiti picked up the handset, pressed the switch on the side and spoke into it. "This is Aureus Lodge receiving, over."

The radio crackled again and a voice said, "This is Reuben at Lewa Conservancy. Is Sam Mwamba there? Over."

With relief, Thabiti handed the radio to Sam.

"Sam here, over."

Thabiti heard Reuben respond, "Sam, one of our guides, who was leading a game drive this evening, spotted a jackal with what looked like a human hand in its mouth. So they followed it and eventually scared it enough to drop the object. They brought it back to me and it is a hand. A woman's, I would say, with a gold wedding band and a diamond engagement ring. Over."

CHAPTER THIRTY-FOUR

Thabiti hugged his arms across his body in the early Monday morning air. It was seven o'clock and he, Sam and Judy had left Aureus Lodge and driven to Lewa Conservancy to meet Reuben and his tracker dogs. They stood in the recently cleared finishing area for the Lewa Marathon.

"I still think we should have told Robert Scott Watson that a woman's hand had been found on Lewa," Thabiti said as he blew into his cupped hands.

"If it is his wife's hand, and we discover foul play, then he will be our lead suspect," replied Judy. She didn't have her uniform with her at the lodge, so instead she was wearing a black fleece with 'Police' embroidered across the back.

"I think it best we keep him out of the way for as long as possible," remarked Sam. He was wearing a green woollen hat, black fingerless gloves, and his large frame was accentuated by his British Army issue camouflage padded jacket.

Reuben and another dog handler appeared around the corner of some thorn bushes and were dragged towards them by two large bloodhound dogs.

Obediently, the dogs sat and looked at Thabiti with an expression of solemn dignity. Their faces appeared to droop because of the excess of wrinkled skin they carried and their long sagging ears.

"Habari," greeted Reuben. He carried a small blue and white cool box. "I suggest we drive to the spot where the hand was found and see if the dogs can pick up the trail back to its source."

Thabiti noted that he avoided saying body.

"Jump in," said Sam. He was driving one of the lodge safari vehicles and he and Reuben climbed into the cab. Thabiti and Judy joined the other handler and the dogs in the back.

As they drove through the open, seemingly empty landscape, Thabiti marvelled at its sheer expanse. It was so different from the busy, noisy Nairobi he knew so well, and even from Nanyuki, which was never quiet. But out here he could almost feel that time was something tangible.

It was extraordinary, as if the past and future came together and were indistinguishable from the present. How many other people, possibly his own ancestors, had gazed across these same plains? In the distance, the Mathews range had, for centuries, watched over the slowly evolving landscape.

The vehicle stopped and Thabiti stepped out onto a dry grassland area beside an umbrella thorn tree. The black earth track beside them was the one he and Marina had run and walked along during the marathon and, looking back, he saw it disappear down a steep hill which had been particularly tiring to walk up.

"I believe this is the spot," said Reuben as he climbed out of the car carrying the cool box. He opened it in front of the dogs, who stuck their long pointed muzzles inside. The leads jerked and Reuben and the other handler were borne away. "Please bring the cool box with you," Reuben shouted over his shoulder.

"They don't seem very sure where to go," commented Judy, as they watched the dogs zigzag across the area in front of them, often doubling back, stopping, sniffing all around and then following another invisible path.

"They're seeking out the right scent," Sam replied. "They should be able to distinguish the scent of the hand from the jackal which carried it, and the other animals that have passed this way, even though it was found yesterday evening."

The other handler's dog barked, and with its nose almost touching the ground, the bloodhound set off back along the side of the track they had driven along.

Sam jumped into the car. "Are you coming with me or walking?"

"I'll walk," replied Judy.

She jogged to catch up with the dogs as Thabiti climbed into the vehicle beside Sam.

He watched the dogs and remarked, "They move at quite a speed."

Sam chuckled. "When they have the scent, little gets in their way. They are invaluable in our anti-poaching efforts and one of the primary reasons Lewa has reduced the number of poaching incidents."

Thabiti ran his fingers across the dashboard in front of him. "But how do they stop the poachers?"

Sam drove steadily along the black earth track. "They don't physically stop them, but they have become so efficient at tracking down the culprits following a poaching incident, often over many miles to outlying villages, that it acts as a great deterrent. You see the gangs need local recruits to steal the ivory and most are now too scared to work for them."

They drove on for over a mile, following the route of the marathon up a hill. They descended into the main valley and Thabiti spotted the dogs turn off the track by a thicket of white thorn acacia trees. Sam parked the car, and they followed the dogs through the trees until they emerged into a small clearing. The dogs began to bark in the undergrowth at the far end.

Reuben pulled them back, turned to Sam and said solemnly, "They have found your body."

Judy stepped carefully through the damaged vegetation and squatted down to examine something. She stood, turned and called to Thabiti, "It's the body of a young woman. Thabiti, do you mind confirming that it's Nina Scott Watson?"

Thabiti felt his chest tightening. Did he really have to identify the body? He looked around the group and found everyone watching him expectantly. What had he thought would happen? They had gone in search of Nina's body and he was the only one who had met her in person.

He took a small, hesitant step forward.

Sam took hold of his arm. "Don't worry. I'll come with you."

Thabiti stopped and looked at him wide-eyed. "I've only seen one dead body. And that was my mother's."

Sam took him firmly by the elbow and guided him forward. "I suspect this one will look less like a living person and more like a corpse, having been out here overnight, and we know she's missing a hand."

Thabiti stopped and bent over, feeling bile rise in his throat. He gulped and looked up at Judy. She gave him a clenched half-smile of pity.

She had no problem examining a dead body, so why should he? He shook himself free of Sam and stepped forward through the trampled undergrowth.

The body was indeed like something from a horror movie with sallow, blotched skin. Not only was the left arm missing, but also her right foot and her eyes. He turned quickly away, not wanting to see any more.

"Yes, that's Nina," he called as he rushed to the entrance of the clearing and vomited.

CHAPTER THIRTY-FIVE

Identifying the dead body of Nina Scott Watson had shaken Thabiti. He sat outside a wooden hut in the security headquarters of Lewa Conservancy, with a red and green shuka wrapped around his shoulders.

Reuben handed him a chipped mug and said, "Some hot, sweet tea should help for the shock. That wasn't very nice. Poor woman."

Thabiti looked across to a silver pickup whose rear tail gate had been lowered. Sam and Judy were examining the bundle protruding from it on a wooden board. He knew it was Nina's body and looked away as he began to shiver.

He wrapped his hands around the mug and drank his tea.

Sam and Judy joined him but remained standing.

"This is a nasty business," said Sam. He looked down at Thabiti and continued, "And I'm sorry you had to be the one to identify the body, but we couldn't wait for Robert Scott Watson to join us. The rising temperature would greatly increase the rate of body decomposition, making it much harder to establish the cause of death."

Thabiti choked on his tea.

Judy patted him on the back and said softly, "Would you rather we discussed this amongst ourselves, without you?"

No, he would not. He looked at the ground and took three long, deep breaths before sitting up and squaring his shoulders. "I want to be part of this investigation. I need to be since Mama Rose is not here."

Sam cleared his throat. "I wasn't aware that Mama Rose was an official member of any investigative force, although I do admit her sleuthing skills have been useful over the past few months."

Reuben reappeared from the wooden hut and handed a mug to Sam.

"Can you put mine on the windowsill?" asked Judy as she removed a notebook and pencil from her fleece pocket. "Let's get on with this. We have the body of Nina Scott Watson, whose identity has been confirmed by Thabiti Onyango." She spoke aloud as she wrote in her notebook.

"The body was found at?"

Sam answered, "07.40 hours on Monday 13th June 2016."

"Thank you." Constable Wachira gave him a grim smile.

"But the hand was found last night," stated Reuben.

The constable picked up her cup. "Of course. And I may need to speak to the guide who spotted it and brought it back, but later." She drank from her mug and replaced it on the wooden windowsill.

"For now, let's try to get a picture of Mrs Scott Watson's movements."

She turned in Thabiti's direction. "The last confirmed sightings of her were by your sister, Pearl, and Julius, from Mount Kenya Wildlife Conservancy, at sunrise yesterday morning. So sometime between six and seven o'clock."

Thabiti nodded.

The constable sucked the end of her pencil and pondered, "So how did she, or her body, end up in a thicket of white thorn acacia trees on Lewa Conservancy?"

"She could have walked along the track we drove back on from the marathon," suggested Thabiti. "It would take her to the finishing area and from there she could have retraced the marathon route."

"But surely someone would have seen her," declared Reuben. "The marathon area was busy yesterday with the competitors who had stayed overnight. And BATUK, the safari companies and our own team were dismantling tents and equipment."

"Perhaps," Sam said slowly and appeared to be considering the point. "But actually that might have made her less conspicuous. Please, can you ask the Lewa crew, and indeed all those on Lewa Conservancy, if they saw an English woman out in the conservancy yesterday?"

"On her own," added Thabiti.

"Not necessarily," mused Sam. "We don't know that she was on her own. She could have met someone. So Reuben, any sighting, although as you pointed out there were still competitors around from the marathon, so I doubt anyone would have taken any notice of her."

Sam sipped from his cup and looked around the security headquarters. "Still, I doubt she walked all that way. It would have taken her a good four or five hours. And a young English woman on her own. It just doesn't add up."

A phone rang inside the hut and a voice shouted, "It's for you Reuben." He disappeared inside to take the call.

Thabiti wrapped the blanket more tightly around himself, looked from Sam to Judy, and asked, "Did you say you don't know what killed her?"

Judy tapped her pencil against her thigh. "No. There were no obvious signs of blunt force trauma."

Sam looked at Thabiti and clarified, "She doesn't appear to have been hit over the head. Well, no injury we could discern from looking at the body, that would have killed her."

Judy continued, "Nor could we find any evidence that she was shot, either by a bullet or an arrow."

"We might be better discussing this back at the lodge," suggested Sam. "And we need to tell Robert Scott Watson that we've found his wife, before he overhears any of the lodge staff discussing the discovery of a body."

Judy glanced back at the pickup. "Shall we have one final examination of the body before we leave?"

Thabiti remained in his seat and tried not to watch Sam and Judy approach the car and lift the shuka blanket off the object in the back.

Reuben reappeared from the hut. "I have to go. The dogs are needed to track down a missing cow at one of the conservancy's neighbouring villages. Do you need anything else?"

Thabiti shook his head.

"Ok. Well, I've spoken to the guide who found the hand, and he is escorting a group to the watering hole below Aureus Lodge this evening for sundowners. Can you let the constable know he'll be there in case she wants to speak to him?"

Thabiti nodded and sipped more tea.

Thabiti sat on the viewing deck outside the living room and slowly ate some buttered toast. He was feeling less queasy. Through the open balcony doors leading into Robert Scott Watson's room, he could hear most of a conversation between Robert and Judy.

"What do you mean you've found her body on Lewa? How could she possibly have got there? I thought she was last seen walking towards the watering hole."

Thabiti thought Robert Scott Watson sounded indignant rather than upset, but perhaps he was also suffering from shock after being told his wife was dead.

"That is what one witness told us. But her body was found this morning on Lewa, and her identity confirmed by Thabiti, one of your lodge managers. Do you know how she got to Lewa?" asked Judy.

"No, of course not," Robert snapped. Then he asked in a matter-of-fact tone, "How did she die?"

"We're not certain. We would like to have an autopsy, but in Kenya the next of kin has to pay for one. Are you happy to authorise and pay for an autopsy?"

Thabiti did not hear Robert's reply.

Judy continued, "Good, we'll get on with that. Do you know anyone in Kenya? Have you any family or friends who could be with you during this upsetting time?"

"I did meet an old friend when we arrived at Nanyuki air strip. But I don't know if she is still around."

"If you give me her details, I'll see if we can find her," responded Judy.

CHAPTER THIRTY-SIX

Rose met Chris at the hospital on Monday morning to visit Craig. She had slept surprisingly well and felt a little guilty that she had enjoyed stretching out and having the bed to herself. She had been joined by Potto, who had curled up on the spot where Craig's feet should have been, and Izzy.

Chris was waiting for her at the bottom of the concrete steps, which led up to the reception area in the recently constructed main hospital building.

"Was it a late one last night?" she asked him.

"Yes, we left Cape Chestnut around eight pm but continued the party at a friend's house." He cradled a white paper disposable cup.

"Will you be staying in our guest cottage tonight?"

"Would you like me to?" He sipped from the cup.

"Of course, but I do understand that as you're only here for a short time, you may have other people to see."

"Shall we?" Chris led the way up the steps. "That's true. I have been trying to get in touch with friends in Timau and the surrounding farms, but I haven't heard back from them yet. Besides, I don't want you to be worried and alone."

"Let's see what the day brings." She opened the door into the hospital reception area.

"Can I see my husband, Craig Hardie?" she asked the bespectacled African woman behind a curved white counter.

The woman consulted a computer and replied, "Yes, the doctor has completed her rounds in that block."

They walked along a corridor, past the doctors' and registrars' consulting rooms, and pushed open a door at the end of the building. They entered a smaller corridor in one of the hospital's older buildings, turned right, strode past several doors and opened the one into Craig's small ward.

Two of the beds were now empty, although the one which the boda boda driver had occupied had the top sheet turned neatly over and looked ready for his return.

She smiled at Craig and kissed him on the forehead. "How are you?" She placed a large brown envelope on the bedside locker.

Craig smiled thinly back at her. "Sore. As well as the damage to my hip, the nurses also discovered a large bruise extending from my shoulder, down my back, and to my hip, which is also likely to be a result of my fall. To be honest, I've mostly slept since I've been in here."

Chris placed a chair next to Craig's bed for Rose and she sat down, taking hold of Craig's translucent hand. "I'm sure that's the best thing for you, and it'll help with the healing process."

Craig looked up at Chris and asked, "What were you up to yesterday? You look rather bleary-eyed."

"I took Mum for lunch at Cape Chestnut and then met up with some mates. It was quite a late night." He rubbed his eyes with his free hand and took another sip from his white disposable cup.

"You know that whilst I'm in here you need to look after your mother," Craig instructed his son.

Rose squeezed Craig's hand and said, "We've already discussed this. Chris will stay at the cottage. But he still has friends to catch up with, and I'm more than capable of spending the night on my own if he's out with friends."

She looked down at the bed, not wanting to add that she might have to get used to being on her own.

"Is Heather coming?" Craig asked in a slightly hoarse voice. Rose stood and passed him a glass of water, which he sipped.

She looked back at Chris.

He responded, "We haven't spoken to her yet. Yesterday was rather busy … "

"And we thought we'd see how you were progressing today and wait for an update from Dr Farrukh," Rose said in a bright voice.

Chris added, "And she's arriving in just under two weeks anyway. But I'll call her once we have an update from your doctor."

The door to the small ward opened and Rose expected to see Dr Farrukh, but instead it was Commissioner Akida carrying a bottle of whisky.

He wore a khaki-coloured uniform with a short-sleeved shirt, a leather cross belt with a shiny gold buckle, and a peaked cap. He removed his cap with his free hand and lodged it under his arm.

"Bwana Hardie. I heard you had been in the wars. What was it? Were you fighting off a lion attack?"

Craig tried but failed to sit up.

The commissioner reached forward with his arm and said in an apologetic tone, "Please, don't move on my account."

Craig rested his head back on the pillows and said, "Commissioner, how good of you to come. Alas, it was just a fall, but I land a little heavier these days than I used to."

"I'd hide that bottle before the nurse sees it," shouted the African man in the bed opposite.

"Good idea." The commissioner placed his cap on the end of Craig's bed and looked round.

Chris stepped across and said, "Let me take that."

Whilst Chris hid the bottle inside the bedside cabinet, Craig said, "That's very good of you. I'm sure my fellow patients and I will enjoy a wee dram on an evening."

"We certainly will," the man in the other bed replied.

"So …" The commissioner looked around, as if unsure what to do or say next.

Rose asked, "Is there any news from Constable Wachira? Did they find Nina Scott Watson?"

"Haven't you heard?" The commissioner looked down at her.

"No," she replied quickly. "What's happened?"

"The Lewa tracker dogs found her body this morning. Young Thabiti identified it, which I believe was rather an unpleasant experience for him."

"Why?" asked Chris, returning to the other side of the bed.

Rose looked across to him and said in a gentle tone, "Because the last dead body he saw was that of his mother, and it was only a few months ago."

The commissioner toyed with his cap. "And this one had been out in the bush overnight and had been disfigured by animals. In fact, the staff at Lewa were only alerted to its presence when a guide spotted a jackal carrying a human hand."

"How awful," remarked Rose. "But why were the Lewa staff involved? Surely the body was found on Borana?"

The commissioner frowned. "That's not what I was told. It was discovered amongst some white thorn acacia trees beside the marathon course, about four kilometres from the finish."

That's strange, Rose thought. Even if Nina had encountered a vehicle at the watering hole, and the driver had given her a lift or kidnapped her, why would she end up in Lewa Conservancy?

She asked the commissioner, "Do you know the cause of death?"

He shook his head. "There is nothing obvious on the body. No signs she was hit or shot. It's another reason for my visit to the hospital this morning. The body arrived here half an hour ago, and an autopsy is currently being conducted."

"Oh, the poor girl. I wonder how her husband is reacting," mused Rose almost to herself.

"Well, he didn't appear particularly upset according to the constable. But she put it down to the shock of finding out his young wife was dead."

"Perhaps, perhaps ..." considered Rose. "I wonder if I should ..."

"Not get involved in this case, Mum. And leave it to the police." Chris crossed his arms and watched her with narrowed eyes.

She swallowed and fidgeted with her hands. Perhaps he was right. That her place was here, by Craig's bedside, and not searching around Borana and Lewa for clues into the death of a girl she barely knew.

"Steady," interjected Craig as he looked up at his son. "I agree that I don't like your mother getting caught up in anything dangerous, but she does seem to have a knack for solving puzzling cases. I'm sure that assisting Commissioner Akida, here in Nanyuki, won't do her any harm. Besides, it might help to keep her mind off ... other things."

The commissioner coughed and said, "Well. It's time I returned to my office. I shall be back later for the results of the autopsy, so I'll pop in again and see how you all are. Bwana, Mama Rose."

He left, and the silence was broken by the ringtone of Rose's phone. She answered it.

"Habari, Mama Rose. Are you back in Nanyuki or are you still in Borana?" Dr Emma, her veterinary colleague and nominal boss, spoke urgently.

"I'm back. Why? Do you have an emergency?"

"Yes. One of the bloodhound tracker dogs is arriving shortly from Lewa. It sounds as if it is bloated, so we'll need to treat it immediately to try to prevent it twisting its gut and dying. Can you assist me?"

"Just a minute," she said into the phone. Was it OK to leave Craig and help Dr Emma? Chris was eyeing her intently and his lips were pressed together.

She conferred with Craig, "Dr Emma has a patient she needs some help with. Do you mind if I go? I shouldn't be more than a few hours."

"Yes, of course, you must go." Craig smiled and looked across at his son. "Chris can keep me company."

"I'm coming," Rose told Dr Emma and ended the call. She looked up at Chris, whose body was tense as he licked his lips.

She stood and collected the brown envelope from on top of the bedside cabinet. "I found some cross-word puzzles. Perhaps you and Craig can work through them whilst I'm away."

"Of course," replied Chris glancing over at the door, and back at his father.

Craig smiled. "I'd enjoy that."

CHAPTER THIRTY-SEVEN

When Rose arrived at Dr Emma's pharmacy, in the centre of Nanyuki, she found Reuben and the distressed bloodhound had already arrived.

Dr Emma did not look like a typical vet. She was petite in stature but everything else about her was large: her afro-style hair, her round yellow glasses and her lips which today were painted a vivid shade of pink.

Neither was the pharmacy a typical veterinary clinic. Inside it looked just like a shop, which indeed it was, as Dr Emma supplemented her veterinary income by selling medicines and animal accessories.

Whenever she needed to operate, or perform a more in-depth examination of a patient, she cleared a white plastic table of its display of dog bowls, cat baskets and a red hamster cage – Rose thought the latter had been on display for at least five years.

The table had been cleared, moved into the centre of the room and covered with clean, but frayed towels. A large placid dog stood uncomfortably on it with his head and long floppy ears drooping forward. A trickle of drool leaked from the corner of his mouth.

Dr Emma prodded his stomach and commented, "Yes, it is certainly hard and swollen."

Rose struggled to put on her white veterinary coat. When Reuben stepped across to help her, she asked him, "What happened?"

"We were searching for a missing cow in one of the villages bordering the conservancy. I noticed that Baz was panting and then he stopped and tried to retch but he didn't vomit. I know that's a sign of bloat as it's very common in bloodhounds. So I drove him straight here to see Dr Emma."

Rose approached the table and asked Dr Emma, "What do we need to do?"

"Pray that we're in time and that we can release the build-up of air and gas with a simple stomach pump." Dr Emma turned to Rueben and confided, "We can't operate here to untwist his gut. If that's happened, he'll need to go to Nairobi. But let's see what we can do."

Dr Emma searched in a cupboard and removed a needle and glass bottle. "It's recommended that stomach pumps are done under a general anaesthetic," she explained, "but again, we don't have the facilities for that. I'm going to give him a sedative instead, which will help ease his pain and discomfort, and make it easier for us to perform the procedure."

She inserted the syringe and needle into the bottle and drew out a measure of liquid. As she turned it over and pushed the plunger to remove the air bubbles she asked, "Can you hold him still, Rose, and if possible, Rueben, can you distract him?"

Baz was now sitting on the table and it was easy for Rose to wrap an arm around his middle. Reuben did the same with his neck, which he gently massaged with his free hand as he whispered in Swahili into the dog's ear.

Dr Emma gripped the top of his thigh to isolate the muscles, inserted the needle and slowly depressed the plunger.

Next to her was a black bucket which held a length of silicone tube, a cloth and a white tub. She smeared some lubricant jelly from the tub around half the length of tube. Then she prised open the bloodhound's mouth, placed the folded cloth between its jaws and inserted the end of the tube.

"Keep him still. This is the difficult part."

Slowly she guided the tube into the dog's mouth and down his oesophagus to his stomach. It stopped, so she pushed a bit harder and another inch of tube entered the dog. Immediately, they heard a hiss of escaping air.

Dr Emma wiped her sweating forehead with the back of her gloved hand. "Great, we're in and we've released the trapped air. He should be more comfortable now, but I think I'll also try to remove the contents of his stomach, just in case there's something in there that caused the bloating."

She sucked on the end of the tube and Rose watched a murky brown liquid rise up through it. Dr Emma spat and winced as she dropped the end of the tube into the bucket.

She strode across to her shop counter, grabbed a bottle of water and swirled some of its contents around her mouth. She spat into the bucket where the water mixed with the viscous liquid from the dog's stomach.

Rose said, "His stomach feels much softer now and less swollen." She looked across at Reuben, who was still whispering to the dog, and asked, "Was this one of the tracker dogs that found the body this morning?"

Dr Emma choked on the water she was drinking and exclaimed, "What body?"

"A young English woman," replied Reuben. "Baz and Blaze found her, poor thing. Wild animals had already started scavenging her body."

CHAPTER THIRTY-EIGHT

R ose returned to the hospital less than two hours after she had left it. She walked into Craig's ward and was relieved to find Chris relaxing by his father's bed, filling in a crossword puzzle.

"Final clue, Dad. Six letters. 'Illegal location for divorce'."

Craig looked up at her, smiled and asked, "Did you save your patient?"

Rose nodded. "Yes, and it was an important one. Baz, one of the tracker dogs from Lewa who found Nina Scott Watson's body this morning."

She remained standing as Chris was poised over the crossword, waiting for an answer.

"Well, it's not Vatican as that's seven letters," considered Craig. "So for six it must be Manila." He lay back on his pillows and screwed up his eyes.

Chris stood and said to Rose, "He needs his painkillers, which I presume will be administered just before or after lunch."

"Lunch," repeated Craig, opening his eyes.

"Not yet, but it'll be here shortly. We better leave so we don't disturb you," responded Chris. His ears turned red as he returned the chair to the corner of the room.

Craig could no longer feed himself and they did not want to get in the way. Rose also thought Chris was embarrassed about his father's incapacity.

Rose bent over Craig and kissed his cheek. "We'll let you have lunch, but I'll be back later."

He reached for her hand and squeezed it. "If you feel you need to help the commissioner, then don't hesitate on my account. I've realised you cannot put your life on hold for me and you will need plenty to do, to keep you going when I'm no longer around." He squeezed her hand again and smiled weakly.

She felt tears prick at the corner of her eyes and she bent down and kissed him again.

As she walked along the stark corridor with Chris, they passed the lunch trolley and the smell of beef stew wafted in their direction.

Rose's stomach growled as she commented, "Your dad should sleep well if he eats stew for lunch. Did you see Dr Farrukh?"

"Yes, but she said it's still too early to determine how well the fracture is healing or when he can return home, if indeed he can." He looked across at Rose. "But I understand a new wing has opened here for elderly patients who need round-the-clock care."

"That's the Louise Decker Centre. It opened quite recently and is a fantastic addition to the hospital. I know a number of elderly and bed-bound patients who are there, so I really should visit them. Why do you mention it?"

"Dr Farrukh suggested we consider it for Dad once he's on the road to recovery from his fall. She said it's brighter, airier and more pleasant than his ward, and at the moment there is space for him."

They stopped and Rose looked down at the floor, rubbing her hands on her thighs.

"What's wrong? Do you want him home? I thought it would be easier for you if he was close by and being cared for in a facility like that."

"It's not that. It's a great idea. But not one I think we can afford."

Chris ran his tongue over his bottom lip and said, "Let's see then. I might be able to help out for a bit."

They walked down the concrete steps at the front of the main hospital building. At the bottom, Chris turned to her and said, "I really need a shower and a rest myself. Will you be all right if I go?"

"I'll keep your mother company," announced Commissioner Akida as he strode towards them. "And I would appreciate her input on a small matter."

Chris pursed his lips and said, "Thank you, Commissioner, but don't drag her into anything dangerous."

The commissioner laughed. "Don't you worry. Anyway, I'm quite sure your mother can look after herself."

Rose looked at Chris and remembered an occasion only two months before when her son had rescued her from certain death. She put a hand on his arm and said, "I promise not to go chasing dangerous criminals on my own."

Chris's shoulders loosened a little, but he still watched her with narrowed eyes as he pecked her on the cheek and said, "Make sure you don't." He walked towards the gravelled visitors' car park.

Rose sighed deeply and turned to Commissioner Akida. "How can I be of assistance?"

"I thought we might visit the mortuary for the results of the autopsy."

They walked between a variety of older single- and double-storey buildings towards the rear of the hospital. As they approached the river, the Louise Decker Centre came into view.

There were pots of flowers and hanging baskets by the entrance, and it certainly looked a pleasant place to stay, but could they afford it? Had Chris genuinely offered to help them financially or did he just feel it was the right thing to say at the time?

"You're unusually quiet, Mama Rose. Is it Bwana Craig? Is he all right?"

They walked around the end of a building, where patio doors led out of a ward onto the grass lawn, and continued towards the mortuary.

"Not really. And Dr Farrukh is not sure he will be well enough to return home. His hip might not heal properly and even if it does, the post-polio syndrome, as they are now calling it, is eating away at his body. He may soon need round-the-clock care."

"I am sorry. Bwana is a proud man, but like all bull elephants, the time finally comes for us to seek out the elephant's graveyard and die in peace."

They entered the single-storey, brick mortuary building. A white-coated pathologist was washing his hands in a stainless-steel sink.

When he saw them, he exclaimed, "Commissioner, I'm glad you're here. I was about to leave for lunch, but first, let me show you my findings."

The commissioner turned to Rose and said, "Brace yourself, the body is a bit of a mess."

"I'm sorry," apologised the pathologist, "I have tried to clean her up, but there are scratches and bite marks from wild animals. Her right foot is missing and her left hand is not attached to the body."

They walked into a small whitewashed room, in the centre of which was a stainless steel trolley draped with a white sheet.

The pathologist pulled on a pair of white latex gloves and lifted the sheet from the body. He said, "As you can see, we have a European woman in her early twenties. She was relatively fit and healthy, with no signs that she drank excessively, or smoked. At first I couldn't find any indication as to the cause of death, but have a look here."

The pathologist lifted her head to expose her neck. "If you look carefully, you can see some small marks. They'll actually become clearer and easier to see as the skin dries out and becomes more transparent."

He rested her head back on the trolley and continued, "I'm afraid her eyes are missing, but if you look at the skin of her eyelids, and under her eyelashes, you can see evidence of pinpoint haemorrhaging."

He stood and declared, "Evidence which points to strangulation, and by the marks on the neck, I would suggest with a thin cord."

The commissioner scratched his own neck and said, "So Nina Scott Watson was murdered."

The pathologist covered Nina's body, stripped off his latex gloves and washed his hands. They all returned to the small office at the entrance to the building. The pathologist approached a desk on which rested a large white plastic bag.

"These are the woman's personal affects." He reached inside and removed a smaller plastic bag, the contents of which he tipped out onto the desk.

Rose picked up a small gold locket. She pushed the clasp at the side to reveal the faces of a middle-aged man and woman. Nina's parents, she presumed. There was also a small gold watch, a silver bracelet, and a couple of beaded bracelets which she presumed Nina had bought whilst in Kenya. Her gold wedding ring and diamond engagement ring lay side by side.

The commissioner looked inside the larger plastic bag and reached in with his hand, moving the objects around.

The pathologist said, "Most of her clothing was ripped or missing, a result of animal scavengers, and there is only a single trainer."

"There's not much to go on," agreed the commissioner. "Were there any traces of blood on the clothes?"

"No, the only fluid I could find evidence of was sweat."

The commissioner's phone rang, and he stepped outside the building to take the call.

Rose thanked the pathologist and followed the commissioner.

CHAPTER THIRTY-NINE

Thabiti, Sam and Judy sat with Marina on the viewing deck outside the drawing room, after eating a late-morning brunch.

"So what's your plan of action for the rest of the day?" Marina asked as she yawned and stretched.

"I'm not sure." Constable Wachira picked up her notebook from the coffee table and flicked through it. "We're waiting to hear back from Reuben as to whether any of the Lewa staff, who were dismantling marathon equipment yesterday morning, saw a lone English woman."

"And the guide who found the hand will be at the watering hole this afternoon," prompted Thabiti.

"I'm not sure what else he will be able to tell us, though," reflected Sam as he sipped his coffee.

Judy's phone buzzed. She removed it from the pocket of her fleece, and said, "Good Morning. Constable Wachira speaking." She listened to the voice at the other end and then spoke. "I'm sorry to hear that. I hope it soon recovers. And pass on our thoughts to Reuben."

"Trouble?" asked Marina sleepily.

"Reuben has rushed one of the tracker dogs to the vet in Nanyuki, and he hasn't had a chance to speak to any of the Lewa staff."

"He'll have taken it to see Dr Emma," commented Thabiti. "I wonder if Mama Rose is helping her. Do you know what was wrong with the dog?"

"Bloat, which is apparently common in bloodhounds, but very serious, and can kill them if not treated quickly."

Marina stretched out her legs and lay back in her chair. "Poor thing. It must be really uncomfortable. Good job bloating is not serious in humans, hey, Thabiti?"

Thabiti fixed his eyes on the wooden decking floor and mumbled, "I don't know what you mean."

Judy stood up. "Well, I might as well interview the staff myself. Are you coming, Sam?"

He rubbed his chin. "Perhaps Thabiti could drive you. While you search for sightings of Nina, I'll concentrate on the car, which we think was parked by the watering hole. I think it more likely she had a lift in it than walked."

Thabiti glanced up at Sam and said, "But won't there have been loads of cars leaving Lewa yesterday morning?"

Sam drained his coffee mug and placed it on the wooden table. "Absolutely, but someone might have noticed something unusual, and there's just a chance the car left by one of the other gates, on Lewa or Borana. I thought I'd drive around and check. Besides, it'll give me a chance to speak with the security guards and discover if there are any local tensions or rumours of any upcoming poaching incidents, and that sort of thing."

"Well, I'm shattered," announced Marina. "I'm going to lie down for a few hours. Robert only wants a light lunch, so the staff can sort him out. I presume you'll both be staying again tonight?"

"If that's OK," Judy replied, leaning on the back of her chair. "I expect it'll be dark by the time Sam finishes his enquiries."

Marina waved a weary hand as she left the viewing deck.

"I better call the commissioner and update him before I go." Judy moved to the edge of the viewing platform to make her call.

Thabiti heard her say, "That changes everything. Will you be joining us at Borana?"

She listened again and then said, "I'm going to interview staff at Lewa and Sam's going to make enquiries about a car which might have been parked near the lodge. Sir, I wondered if you could send someone to BATUK to question the staff who were dismantling tents yesterday at the marathon. We need to find out if any of them saw a woman fitting Mrs Scott Watson's description, or anything else that they thought was unusual."

She listened and then asked, "Have you had any luck finding Mr Scott Watson's friend Vivian Scott?" After a short pause she responded, "Still making enquiries. OK."

She finished the call and turned to stare at the balcony of Robert Scott Watson's room. Looking back at Sam and Thabiti she inclined her head, and said in a hushed voice, "Follow me."

She crossed the drawing room and closed the door to the hall. As Thabiti stepped inside from the viewing deck she asked, "Can you shut that door as well?"

Sam strode across to stand in front of Judy, and asked, "What is it? What did the commissioner tell you?"

She gulped, looked straight at him, and said, "Nina Scott Watson was murdered. Strangled, according to the pathologist who conducted the autopsy."

Thabiti collapsed into an armchair and murmured into his hands, "Oh the poor woman."

Sam responded, "It's more important than ever then that we make our enquiries before the trail runs cold."

Thabiti closed his eyes and massaged his forehead. "I bet it was her husband."

Sam turned to him, "But how could it have been? You said he was here in the lodge all of yesterday."

"He was, but I still think he did it."

Sam turned back to Judy. "Are you going to tell him that his wife was murdered?"

She pinched the top of her nose and answered, "No. I don't think so. Not yet, anyway. If he was involved, then he'll already know, and I think it best we keep him in the dark about our investigation for a long as possible. And if he wasn't involved, it might be best to wait and see if his friend arrives before breaking the news."

"When will she get here?"

"The commissioner hasn't found her yet, so I'm not sure."

Sam gave her a hug and announced, "Well, we better get started. Thabiti, you're driving Judy to Lewa. Make sure you look after her."

"I'm quite capable of looking after myself."

"I know you are, my dear, but it's always prudent to have backup."

CHAPTER FORTY

As Rose left the mortuary, her phone rang. She answered it and heard Julius say, "Habari, Mama Rose. How is Bwana Hardie?"

"Habari Julius. He is comfortable in the Cottage Hospital. He damaged his hip in the fall, as I suspected, and we shall have to wait to see how well it heals."

"Again, I am so sorry Mama." He sounded dejected.

"Julius, it is not your fault, and you were tired after being out all night with the jackals. How are they, by the way?"

Rose began to walk across the lawn, away from the mortuary.

"That was the reason for my call, Mama. I thought they would have left their enclosure by now and settled in the main conservancy. I opened the enclosure gate on Saturday night and two did venture outside. Last night three left the enclosure, but one female stayed inside. And I've lost the male who didn't return this morning. I'm not sure what to do and I need to return to the orphanage soon."

Rose sat down on a wooden bench. She suddenly felt exhausted. "But you are staying tonight and watching them?"

"Yes, but can you join me?" Julius beseeched.

Rose felt wretched about letting Julius down as she said, "I'm sorry, I'm not sure I can tonight. I need to be here for Craig."

"Of course. I understand, Mama." He sounded disappointed.

"Call me in the morning and let me know if the fourth jackal returned. But I'm not sure what we can do if it doesn't, and the others refuse to leave their enclosure."

She finished the call and sighed as she looked up at Mount Kenya through a gap in the trees. There was no sign of clouds and the beneficial effects of the long rains in April and early May were diminishing as the recent growth of grass turned yellow. Nearby, the Nanyuki river trickled along its rocky base.

Commissioner Akida sat down next to her and asked, "Are you trying to solve this puzzle of a crime?"

"Sorry?" Rose responded in confusion.

"Nina Scott Watson's death. It's quite a riddle."

Rose turned to the commissioner and said, "I'm sorry, but my mind was elsewhere. I haven't had a chance to think about your case. Was that call related to it?"

The commissioner leaned back on the bench. "Yes, Constable Wachira was providing an update. She's going to interview the staff at Lewa who were dismantling the marathon tents and structures yesterday, to establish if there were any sightings of Nina Scott Watson. And Sam is trying to trace a car."

Rose closed her eyes. "That will probably be the one we think was parked near the watering hole. Nina's hat was found nearby. So what will you do now?"

"The constable asked me to send someone to BATUK and interview the staff who were also at the marathon yesterday. And what about you, Mama?"

She turned to look at him. "I've no idea, Commissioner. I don't know which direction to turn."

The commissioner patted her on the shoulder and strode away. What should she do now? Her stomach rumbled, but she didn't really feel like eating a large meal. Sometimes there was a lady in the visitors' car park who sold samosas.

She pushed her weary body off the bench and wandered through the hospital grounds to the car park. A large African woman sat on the kerb next to what looked like a wheelbarrow, on top of which someone had built a glass-fronted warming unit. There were two piles of golden triangular-shaped samosas inside.

"Habari. Meat or vegetable?" the woman asked.

"Um, one of each, tafadhali." Rose exchanged a hundred-shilling note and a twenty-shilling coin for a brown paper bag. She retraced her steps to the bench in the hospital grounds close to the river.

She bit into a samosa: it was the vegetable one with pieces of carrot, potato and peas, and it was flavoured with fresh coriander.

She felt both trapped and disorientated. She knew it was important to spend time with Craig whilst he recovered from his fall. But what about afterwards? Could they afford for him to stay at the Louise Decker Centre.

She doubted the small contribution the state healthcare policy would pay towards Craig's current hospital stay would extend to long-term care. And they hadn't been able to afford the increasing premiums to continue their healthcare plan after Craig retired.

Unless Chris was willing to pay the majority of the cost, and she wasn't sure he would be or even had the funds to do so, she and her staff would need to look after Craig at home.

Samwell had been wonderful helping Craig, and Kipto was efficient and always prepared to do what was needed, but what happened when Craig deteriorated and was bedridden?

Would he be content spending his final days staring at the walls and ceiling of their bedroom? She was certain he benefitted from fresh air and sitting out on the patio. But what happened when he could no longer do that? Would he just fade away?

And how did she feel about being tied to a dying man? On the one hand, she would relish the chance to sit with him, knowing that their time together was precious, but she also knew herself.

If she was bound to his bedside, unable to continue her veterinary work, or assist the police and her friends, she would certainly become restless by the inactivity and lack of daily achievement. She might even start to resent Craig, which was the last thing she wanted to do.

And what about Chris? He appeared to be on better terms with his father but was he feeling aggrieved towards her? She could understand his unwillingness for her to assist the police since he had been the one to rescue her a few months previously when a deranged killer had tried to drown her.

But even so, she felt under pressure from him to spend every minute of the day with Craig, as if that was her role as a dutiful wife. Yet Craig himself understood how important her work was and her need to help others.

It was probably the result of the forty years of guilt she had carried around for believing she'd killed a poacher. And Dr Emma couldn't tend to all the sick and injured animals in Laikipia on her own.

She felt Chris needed to spend some time with his father, especially as they'd hardly spoken for the last fifteen years. But then she supposed Chris must have a mix of emotions since their reunion two months ago.

She had nearly been killed and his father had suffered a mini-stroke and was terminally ill. She must remember this and try to be more tolerant as she certainly didn't want to fall out with Chris again, not now. But she would have to tread carefully.

She heard someone's phone ring, and then felt a vibration in her trouser pocket. It was her phone. Her heart began to race. Had something happened to Craig?

She grabbed it from her pocket, nearly dropped it and without looking at the caller ID cried, "Hello", into the phone.

"Rose, are you OK?" She heard Chloe's concerned voice.

"Oh, yes. Sorry. You caught me deep in thought and I panicked, thinking that something had happened to Craig."

"I'd better not bother you then." Chloe's tone was apologetic.

"No, I promise I'm all right. Why did you call?"

"It doesn't matter now. It's just that I was speaking to Marina earlier and she invited me to the lodge for the night. I need a break away from Dan and a bit of time by myself to think. Anyway, she said Julius was fretting about some jackals and you not being there. I don't know what it's all about, but I said I was happy to give you a lift if you'd like one."

"Thanks, that's very kind, but I'm not sure I can leave Craig overnight, and he'll certainly want me with him in the morning."

"Well, if it helps I have to be back by eleven for an appointment. It's with the counsellor but I'm not sure Dan will be coming. He got really defensive when I suggested it, and that's the main reason I want to get away for the night."

"That's probably a good idea," responded Rose distractedly.

"Let me know if you change your mind. I was hoping to leave in an hour or so but I'm waiting to hear back from Marina, and find out if I need to drive a friend of Robert Scott Watson's out to the lodge. Apparently the police are looking for her."

CHAPTER FORTY-ONE

T habiti and Judy were directed by a Lewa security guard towards an encampment of round mud huts with dried grass and reed roofs.

As they approached, three chickens, which had been quietly pecking at the ground, squawked and ran off, flapping their wings, pursued by a naked toddler.

A woman backed out of the doorway of one of the huts. She was bent double and flicked a brush, made from a bundle of reeds, to and fro as she swept the dry earth floor.

Thabiti followed Judy, who strode purposely towards a group of men sitting on upturned crates and sections of tree trunks.

"Good afternoon. I'm Constable Wachira, from Nanyuki police station. I understand you were working at the marathon site yesterday morning."

A man with a scar above his left eye looked up at her, squinting in the sunlight and responded, "Is this about the woman's body Baz and Blaze found this morning?"

"Yes it is. And the young woman was murdered, hence my enquiries." Judy stood with a straight back and her feet close together.

The man shook his head and murmured to his friends, "Bad business. And bad for business."

A thick-set man looked up, shielding his eyes with his hand, and asked, "What do you want to know from us?"

Constable Wachira stepped closer and removed her notebook from her trouser pocket. "Well, to start with, did you see a lone English woman wandering through the conservancy, or near the marathon track yesterday morning?"

The men in the circle all shook their heads as they considered the bare earth.

The thick-set man said, "We get plenty of crazy mzungus around marathon time. You had one on Friday night, didn't you?" He nudged his friend, a younger man with a gold earring.

The man with the scar looked at him and said, "Do you mean the woman whose car had broken down in Borana?"

"Tell me about it," prompted the young constable.

The man looked at her shyly, bit his bottom lip and said, "You see, my boss got this call. Apparently some English woman had decided to take a shortcut through Borana to reach the marathon, rather than using the main road. But she'd taken a wrong turn, got herself lost, and then her car had broken down. I was sent to collect her."

"And where was this?" asked Judy as she sucked the end of her pen.

"Below that new lodge, near the watering hole where they've built a viewing platform. Mind you, I never saw the car. I just picked her up and brought her back here."

Thabiti shuffled forward and cleared his throat. The men looked at him and he felt the heat rise in his face as he asked hesitantly, "Was it a young woman wearing a floppy hat, or with fair hair cut quite short?"

The stocky man nudged the younger one again and cried, "Oh no. This one was quite a looker, wasn't she?"

The younger man drew in the earth with his finger but said nothing.

The stocky man grinned at Thabiti. "She had long glossy dark hair and moved like a cheetah."

CHAPTER FORTY-TWO

Rose sat on the bench outside the Cottage Hospital. She felt a knot tightening in her stomach and a tightness in her head.

There were so many things she should be doing, and people who needed her help, but she didn't know what to do. And yet her indecision meant she was achieving nothing.

She felt guilty about leaving Julius alone with his jackal project at Borana, and deep down she realised she missed not being in the centre of the murder investigation.

If Craig slept all afternoon would he even realise she wasn't there? That wasn't fair and she would feel guilty for leaving him alone. He should have finished his lunch now, so she should go back and check on him.

Rose pulled back a small curtain which covered a window in the door to Craig's room. She presumed it was there so staff could check on their patients without disturbing them. Craig was already asleep. Rose ignored the sound of approaching footsteps as she watched his still form.

"You can go in," Dr Farrukh said beside her.

"I don't want to disturb him when he's sleeping."

"I doubt he is as a nurse has just been in to give him his medication. She asked me to come back and look at the bruise on his back. She's concerned it's spreading, but I'm afraid that even if it is, there's little I can do."

Dr Farrukh opened the door and ushered Rose inside.

Craig opened his eyes and smiled.

Dr Farrukh quickly and efficiently examined Craig's back. She straightened up and said, "I don't think there's anything to worry about at the moment. I'll check on you again this evening. Bye, Rose," she said as she left the room.

Rose's face was flushed and she felt hot, and even though she doubted it was the temperature of the room she still said, in a flustered voice, "It's warm in here, isn't it?" She glanced around uncertainly.

Craig tried to lift himself higher on the bed but was unable to do so.

She rushed across to help him. 'Here, let me do that," and she reached out with her hand.

Craig caught hold of her wrist and in a deliberate, but soothing tone asked, "Rose, what's the matter?"

She slumped into a chair which had been left beside Craig's bed. "It's just that … I'm not sure … you see …"

Craig lifted his hand and Rose stopped.

"Shall we begin again?' He asked quietly.

Rose's words gushed out. "My dear, I just don't know what to do. I know I should spend time with you, I want to spend time with you, but I feel guilty, and hopeless, and I can't help other people when they need me. And what happens when you get better and come home? Do I need to sit by your bed all day, in case something happens? And what if I leave you and something does happen?"

"Stop," said Craig firmly, and the African man in the bed opposite opened his eyes and cried out, and then returned to sleep.

"I have never expected you to hold a vigil by my bedside. In fact you would drive me mad as you'd be fretting and wondering what your were missing. It is the quality of our time together, not the quantity, which is important. And how could you tell me the local Nanyuki news, or stories of your patients, if you never left my bedside?"

Rose felt an unexpected release of tension in her body although her head still ached.

Craig continued, "I think Chris has been winding you up about rushing around rather than sitting quietly with me. Don't worry, I'll speak to him and explain that you need to be out and about. And that the local community is important to you. And you to the community."

Rose looked at him gratefully.

Craig yawned. "I'm sorry. I think a combination of lunch and painkillers is kicking in. I think I'll sleep most of the afternoon. Is there something you want to do?"

Rose looked down and began to wring her hands. "There is, but it'll probably keep me away until the morning."

Craig smiled, "That shouldn't be a problem. Dr Farrukh and her team are providing excellent care and there's nothing more you can do for me. I'm not going anywhere. I just need to rest and heal."

She turned and reached forward grasping his hand. "Are you sure?"

"Of course I am. What do you need to do?"

"Return to Borana with Chloe. Julius needs my help with the jackals and, well, you know me," she grinned sheepishly, "I want to know what is happening with Nina Scott Watson's case."

"Of course you do," chuckled Craig, "And I want to hear all about it in the morning."

Rose stepped out of Craig's room and called Chloe. "Have you left yet?"

"No, but the police have spoken to Robert Scott Watson's friend and I'm picking her up at Kongoni's in half an hour."

"If I go home and pack my overnight bag, and check on the animals, can you pick me up?"

"Yes, of course," Chloe replied brightly.

Rose returned to Craig's room but he was already asleep. She kissed his forehead and murmured, "I love you."

CHAPTER FORTY-THREE

An hour after her call, Chloe parked outside Rose's cottage in her black Land Cruiser. Rose carried a small canvas overnight bag and a green canvas tote bag, into which she had remembered to put her glasses, as well as her phone and other items.

"Ready?" asked Chloe as she stepped out of the car and took Rose's overnight bag. She stowed it in the boot of the car and said, "The police found Robert's friend Vivian. So we're picking her up from Kongoni's."

They drove out of Nanyuki, past the agricultural showground which doubled up as BATUK's headquarters, and turned right.

The guard raised the barrier at the entrance to Kongoni's camp and they drove down a track and parked by a single-storey building, whose whitewashed concrete walls did not have a single straight line.

A glamorous dark-haired woman waited outside, tapping her foot. She wore a bright red dress and carried a wide-brimmed straw sunhat.

Chloe got out of the car and Rose heard her ask, "Are you Vivian?"

Both women were tall and attractive and Rose thought they looked like two wild horses, with their flowing manes of glossy hair. As they came face-to-face, each seemed to evaluate the other.

"Ye-es," the woman dragged out the word in a condescending tone. "And you must be Chloe."

Chloe replied, "We met here on Sunday, didn't we? You came and joined me in the pool?"

"Did we? I can't remember." Vivian looked bored and shifted her gaze away from Chloe.

Chloe returned to the car with a pinched expression.

Vivian looked down at her bag, shrugged, picked it up and walked around to the passenger's side. She jumped back when she saw Rose and her eyes widened. She quickly opened the rear passenger door and settled herself and her bag on the rear seats.

Chloe drove out of Kongoni's and turned right towards Timau. There was an uncomfortable silence.

Rose took the opportunity to text Chris. When she'd finished, she stuffed her phone back into her tote bag. Chris would probably be appalled that she had left Craig and gone to Borana, and she didn't want to hear a ping alerting her to his reply.

Finally, Vivian introduced herself, "Hi, I'm Vivian Scott." Her voice was less harsh and had taken on a warmer tone, but somehow she still made the statement sound superior.

Chloe answered, "This is Rose. Our friends, Thabiti and Marina are managing the lodge where we're all staying. I've just thought. It's quite a coincidence that your surname is Scott and the lady who died was called Scott Watson. They're not common names in Kenya."

"Which is actually a surprise," mused Vivian. "As there are many Europeans here whose ancestors arrived from Scotland, and they have names like Murray and Kennedy."

"Or Hardie, like my own," commented Rose.

Chloe slowed for a speed bump, and asked, "Were Craig's parents from Scotland?"

Rose turned to her. "They were, but Craig wasn't born here. He left Scotland in 1970 and moved here for a job. We met, got married, and this became his home."

"How sweet," cooed Vivian in a patronising tone.

Chloe turned to Rose and asked, "What is the lodge like?"

"Stunning," replied Rose. "It's constructed from local stone and has steep pitched thatched roofs. Most of the furniture is antique, which must have been imported, and it's very tastefully decorated with some striking artwork.

"It's rather fitting, considering that some orphan jackals are being rehabilitated close to the lodge, that a new painting, which the owners sent from the UK, is of a family of jackals. But I can't remember the artist's name."

"Annabel Pope," muttered Vivian in the back.

"That's right," agreed Rose.

"Oh, she's painted some wonderful pictures," Chloe said. "I recently saw one with three running ostriches in bright reds and greens and she'd captured their movement so well."

There was silence again.

CHAPTER FORTY-FOUR

Rose invited Sam and Constable Wachira to her room before supper. Thabiti unfolded two wooden safari chairs and arranged them by the room's wingback armchairs.

He turned to Sam and Constable Wachira, and asked, "What would you like to drink?"

"A Tusker for me," replied Sam.

"Just a diet coke, please, as I want to stay alert this evening," said Constable Wachira.

He looked over at Rose, who was unpacking her toiletry bag. "And for you, Mama Rose?"

"A small glass of white wine would be lovely," she replied with a smile.

Sam sat down in an armchair and Constable Wachira in a safari chair. Sam asked Rose, "How is Craig?"

"He's comfortable in the Cottage Hospital and getting the care he needs. But the doctor is not sure how well his hip will heal, or whether there will be any secondary complications."

"I'm sorry," said Constable Wachira. "I hope he's not in too much pain."

Rose thought of Craig lying in his hospital bed and she hoped he was resting peacefully. Despite the tragic end to the weekend, and his fall, she thought he had enjoyed his visit to Borana and the chance to be involved in the Lewa Marathon, if only as a spectator.

Thabiti returned with a tray of drinks, which he set down on the small coffee table.

Rose crossed the room and sat down in the free armchair and enquired, "Did you find out anything useful today about Nina Scott Watson's disappearance and death?"

Sam poured his Tusker into a glass and said, "You go first, Judy."

"There's not much to tell, is there Thabiti?"

Thabiti shook his head as he picked up another bottle of Tusker and moved across to the window.

The constable continued, "The problem is Lewa was full of people on Sunday morning, when Mrs Scott Watson went missing, and none of the Lewa staff noticed anything unusual."

"What about the men from BATUK?" enquired Rose.

"Sergeant Sebunya questioned them. Although they didn't leave Lewa until three o'clock in the afternoon, they didn't see anyone matching Mrs Scott Watson's description. In fact, nobody has."

Thabiti continued to stare into the gathering gloom as night fell. He commented, "The only mzungu woman who was spotted on her own was completely different."

Rose turned to the window and asked sharply, "What do you mean?"

Thabiti turned towards her and then looked down at the floor.

"Sorry, I shouldn't have mentioned it. It happened on Friday night, so it has no bearing on the case."

"What did?" Rose's eyes drew together.

"An attractive mzungu woman, with dark hair, had to be rescued from somewhere near the watering hole. Apparently she was taking a shortcut through Borana to Lewa, got lost, and then her car broke down.

"She had to call the camp where she was staying before the marathon and one of the Lewa staff was sent to collect her." Thabiti picked at the label on his Tusker bottle.

"I had a bit more luck," Sam announced. "I checked the logs of all Borana's entrance gates for Sunday and found an interesting entry. Early, around half past seven on Sunday morning, a female driver exited through the gate onto the Ngare Ndare Forest road. She signed her name as Jane Smith."

Thabiti sighed, "That's not much help. I bet she made the name up. It's like calling myself John Otieno."

Rose asked, "Did the askari remember what she looked like?"

Sam replied, "It was a different guard on duty that day, but we called him. He said he didn't get a good look at the woman as she had a scarf wrapped around her head and was wearing dark glasses."

There was a knock at the door and Chloe poked her head into the room. "Do you mind if I join you?"

"Come in," said Rose. "I see you have a drink. We were just discussing the progress that has been made into the disappearance of Nina Scott Watson. At the moment there just seem to be a lot of dead ends." She turned back to Sam and asked, "Did the gate askari say anything else?"

"The guard who had been on duty thought there was something distinctive about the car, and when we looked at the log, we noted that he had jotted down 'green beetle'."

Rose rubbed her chin and said, "I wonder what he meant by that? Perhaps he saw an unusual bug on the car, but it doesn't help us much."

Chloe sat down on the end of the bed and said in a thoughtful tone, "It could mean a green Beetle car. I saw one in the car park at Kongoni's when we left on Sunday. I noticed it because it was one of the old-style Beetles, and looked as if it had been well cared for, although its shiny green paintwork was covered in dust."

There was another knock on the door and a male voice announced, "Dinner's about to be served."

CHAPTER FORTY-FIVE

Marina stood behind a chair at the end of the dining table closest to the door. Robert and Vivian were already seated on the far side of the table. Their heads were bowed as they conversed in hushed tones. They looked up as Rose and her friends entered.

Marina said in a business-like tone, "Rose, why don't you take the seat at the far end of the table and Sam, can you sit next to her."

Rose and Sam moved and stood behind their respective chairs.

Marina tapped the chair on her right. "Judy, if you sit here, next to Vivian. Chloe next to Sam, and Thabiti," she turned to him, "if you sit between Chloe and myself, then you are close to the door in case anything needs fetching."

The door opened and three uniformed members of staff carried in their starters. They placed plates of smoked trout pate, garnished with salad and served with toast, in front of the diners.

Rose looked down at the table and asked, "Do you mind if I say grace? I feel we need to thank God and ask for his blessing."

Marina smiled, "Of course, what a super idea." She closed her eyes and bowed her head.

Rose closed her eyes and clasped her hands together as she prayed.

"God our Father, thank you for your love and favour. Bless this food and drink and all who share it with us today. May you have mercy on those of us who have sinned, and bless those who we have sinned against. And remember and bless those who are not here to share this meal with us. Amen."

There was a murmur of 'Amens' around the table and then everyone began to eat.

Marina finished her first mouthful and addressed Chloe, "You met Vivian on the journey here, and I think you know everyone else. But can I introduce you to Robert Scott Watson?"

Chloe looked across at Robert, smiled and said, "Nice to meet."

"Likewise," he responded, raising a wine glass in her direction and appraising her with interest. Rose noticed Vivian's face tighten.

Sam asked, "Robert, how long have you two been friends?"

Robert turned to Vivian and placed a hand on her arm. "Oh years, fifteen, or maybe twenty, isn't it?"

"Something like that," Vivian responded sourly.

Robert ignored her and addressed his fellow diners. "I went to work in Manila, in the Philippines. Nothing glamorous, mostly back room auditing and checking company accounts. Vivian's father was in charge of the office.

"Now I'm not sure how many of you have visited the Philippines, but they have the most magnificent beaches, and with over seven thousand islands, some of the best scuba diving in the world."

Vivian's face relaxed, and she exclaimed, "Oh, it's beautiful. So many wonderful coral reefs and gardens, with huge shoals of brightly coloured fish ..."

"And even the odd rare manta ray and whale shark." Robert and Vivian gazed at each other intently, as if sharing a captivating memory.

"And then I left the Philippines to work on a yacht, and a little later, you returned to London," reminisced Vivian.

"But we do bump into each other in the most unusual places," laughed Robert as he turned back to face Sam.

Vivian lifted her chin and looked at Robert with narrowing eyes.

Robert swallowed a large mouthful of red wine and said, "Was it two years ago, no three last February, when we bumped into each other at the Jardin de la Mer, after skiing in Val d'Isère?"

Vivian straightened her jacket and looked a little uncomfortable but was spared from responding as the lodge staff entered to clear away the starter plates.

CHAPTER FORTY-SIX

At a quarter to six on Tuesday morning, Kennedy, Aureus Lodge's gardener, drove Rose and Julius to the jackal enclosure. Julius and Kennedy appeared to have become firm friends.

Rose was delighted that the lodge kitchen had provided them with a flask of hot water, sachets of tea, coffee, milk, sugar and some hot breakfast rolls.

The headlights of the car lit up the enclosure and Rose spotted a lone jackal pacing along the inside of the fence.

"That one is very shy and I don't think she has left the enclosure at all," said Julius in a resigned tone.

"Won't she be hungry?" Kennedy asked.

"Probably, but she will have been eating insects and berries in the enclosure, and even grass. But there will come a point when she is forced to leave to find more food," Julius told him.

Kennedy parked a short distance away from the enclosure, and Rose stepped out into the chilled air. She shivered as she heard the deep roar of a lion. She waited for her eyes to adjust to the darkness and realised that it wasn't pitch black.

A sea of stars, so often obstructed by light pollution from towns and cities, lit up the clear night sky.

"Shall we see if we can find the other jackals?" asked Julius.

Rose and Julius wandered past the enclosure towards the foot of the escarpment, which loomed up like a dark shadow in front of them.

"There," whispered Julius. He pointed to the left, and Rose was able to discern the shadowy shapes of two jackals trotting through the grass.

"I think they're heading back to the enclosure," she said. They followed the jackals back to their starting point.

As Kennedy poured hot water into three mugs, Julius said, "This doesn't look good. We still have only three of them and they are refusing to leave the enclosure."

Rose swirled a tea bag around her cup and replied, "If you need to go back to the orphanage, perhaps Kennedy could keep a watch on the jackals, or someone from Borana. But at some stage the enclosure will have to be dismantled."

She leant against the safari vehicle and sipped her tea. The mounds of hills and silhouettes of bushes and acacia trees were emerging as early morning light seeped into the darkness.

Suddenly they heard a high-pitched cry. Rose heard it again, as if the caller was yowling 'where' into the morning air.

"Look," exclaimed Julius.

The three jackals in the enclosure had turned towards the sound and stood with their ears pricked. One lifted its head to the sky and responded with a similar call. It left the enclosure, and the others followed.

"Quick, get in. We must follow them," shouted Julius.

Rose flung the remains of her tea to the ground and heaved herself into the car's front passenger seat. They moved forward slowly, without lights, following the three jackals. Their route took them out into the conservancy and they were able to drive along a dirt road, keeping the three jackals to their right.

After about a mile and a half the jackals veered right and they followed, with Kennedy carefully negotiating the uneven ground.

Julius, who was leaning forward between the front seats, said urgently, "Steady, there's something up ahead."

Rose began to make out the form of a fourth jackal standing by the side of a partially eaten animal carcass, which she thought was that of a zebra. She wondered if it was killed by the lion she had heard earlier. The lone jackal called again and the other three trotted towards it. They all began to pick at the carcass.

"So the missing jackal had left in search of food," stated Julius.

"Is it true that jackals have their own unique calls which only members of their family respond to?" asked Kennedy.

"Yes, that's correct," replied Julius.

They watched the jackals for twenty minutes, until the four animals stopped and looked warily to their left.

"I think another animal is interested in the carcass," whispered Julius.

They watched as two large hyenas sloped their way towards the jackals. The jackals made half-hearted barks at the hyenas and then turned and trotted back in the direction they had come from.

"They were sensible not to pick a fight with hyenas. And they should have had enough time to fill their bellies," commented Rose.

Kennedy turned the car back to the track, and they followed the jackals. But instead of heading towards the enclosure, they continued towards the base of the rocky escarpment.

"Do you think they found the den?" Julius asked excitedly.

A few minutes later, the jackals disappeared down the sandy hole Julius had shown Rose on their first visit.

"A happy ending," she declared. "Your jackals are reunited."

CHAPTER FORTY-SEVEN

After breakfast at the lodge, Chloe drove Rose back to Nanyuki.

"I thought your friend Julius wanted a lift," commented Chloe.

"He's coming back later with one of the lodge cars, which is doing a supply run to Nanyuki. He's meeting someone from Borana this morning to discuss the removal of the enclosure and the ongoing monitoring of the four jackals."

Rose turned to Chloe and asked, "Did you enjoy your night away?"

"It was great, and the lodge is amazing. I wish I could have stayed longer, and I probably would have if it wasn't for this morning's counselling session."

"What are you going to say to Dan? How will you persuade him to join you?"

"I really don't know. I could either take the helpless, pleading approach. Something along the lines of 'I really need your help', 'this is important to me', that sort of thing. Or I could just issue an ultimatum and tell him that if he refuses to support me, and would prefer to be with his mates, then I'm leaving. But I'm not sure I'm ready to go nuclear just yet."

"I think you're right. Better to err on the side of caution," Rose said as Chloe drove close to the edge of the road to navigate around a particularly large pothole. Rose looked down at the steep drop to the forest floor and wished she hadn't.

Chloe steered back into the middle of the road and continued, "I had a good chat with Marina yesterday, about her family. Did you know they're refusing to talk to her at the moment? And it's all because she refused to see some

Indian man her father arranged for her to meet. She came up to Laikipia instead to manage the lodge."

Chloe slowed down, and the car bumped over the uneven road. "Anyway, she helped me get some perspective on families and relationships."

"Perhaps there is a middle way," suggested Rose. "You could just be completely honest with Dan. And tell him what's troubling you and the concerns you have about your marriage.

"Remind him that there are two people in it and unless he engages, it will fall apart. Then suggest he comes and meets the counsellor, and if he is not happy he can leave. But, for the sake of both of you, please can he give it a try."

Chloe was silent as she drove across a particularly rough section of the Ngare Ndare road. As they emerged under the elephant wire into Ethi village, she said, "I think you're right. It's time to be honest but sincere. And I can't force my marriage to work. Dan has to want it to as well."

Chloe dropped Rose at the Cottage Hospital.

"Thank you, and good luck," called Rose as she shut the car door.

She turned towards the main hospital building, took a deep breath, and braced her shoulders. She picked up her overnight bag and climbed the concrete steps.

When she opened the door into Craig's ward, she found Chris already sitting by his father's bed. He turned to her, folded his arms across his chest and said in an off-hand tone, "Hi Mum. Glad you could join us."

Rose felt her jaw clench, but she steadied herself and said in a friendly tone, "Morning Chris. Thank you for coming to see your father this morning." She walked across to Craig and pecked him on the cheek. "How are you feeling?"

"I'm not sure. The pain seems to be less, but everything is a little numb."

"I'm not surprised," responded Chris. "You've been lying in bed for nearly two days."

Chris got up and found a second chair, which he placed on the opposite side of the bed for Rose. He asked, "So how was Borana?"

"Julius from the Animal Orphanage is a relieved man," she said.

"The jackals," gasped Craig as he tried to shift position. "Tell me all about them."

"Dad, are you OK?" asked Chris.

Craig settled back on his pillows. "Yes, I am now. Go on, Rose." But his face was pale.

"Julius was worried, as one jackal had left the enclosure, and not returned, but the others were reluctant to venture out. Anyway, when we were watching them this morning, we heard a cry and they left. We followed them to a recent kill and the missing jackal.

"After they had eaten, they were chased off by a couple of hyenas, but they didn't return to the enclosure and appear to have taken up residence in an empty den. Julius is going to ask the Borana staff to keep an eye on them as he has to return to the orphanage."

"That's a relief," said Craig. "I'd say a job well done. And what about Thabiti and Marina? How are they getting on?"

"Thabiti's happy enough, especially as Sam and Constable Wachira are staying at the lodge, but Marina seems tired and under pressure."

"I guess that's no surprise, since one of her first guests disappeared and turned up dead," said Craig ruefully. "Is the husband still staying at the lodge?"

"Yes, and Chloe gave his friend a lift yesterday. Do you remember the lady who disembarked from the Lewa flight when we met you, Chris? At the Nanyuki airstrip. She was the elegant, rather ostentatious woman who gave her hat to Nina Scott Watson."

Chris nodded.

"It seems she and Robert Scott Watson have been friends for years, and plenty more besides, I suspect." Rose raised her eyebrows.

"So what is this case all about?" asked Chris.

"Why? Is it starting to interest you?" Rose teased.

"Even I have to admit it's sounds rather fascinating. A missing wife, a non-plussed husband and his attractive 'friend'. And all set in a luxury lodge in a Kenyan wildlife conservancy. It's like a film script."

Rose outlined the facts of the case and the lack of progress in trying to solve it.

Chris leaned back and closed his eyes. He muttered, "I've heard of something similar before. An unsolved case, but where was it?"

Rose waited patiently, intrigued by Chris's interest.

Chris sat up. "That's it. My final inter-services skiing competition before I left the army."

"Skiing," questioned Craig. "I didn't know you could ski. We could never afford those school trips."

"I know," chuckled Chris. "It was one of the reasons I jumped at the chance when the army offered it. Mind you, I think they expected people who actually knew how to ski when they asked for volunteers for a month's training, followed by the inter-services ski challenge."

"How did you get on?" asked Rose.

"The first year was hard, particularly the downhill skiing, and there were plenty better than me. But I was fit, and I can shoot well, so I specialised in the biathlon. And over the years I improved and even competed for the slalom team as well."

"Anyway, what has skiing got to do with this case?" asked Rose in confusion.

"As I was saying. During our trip a woman went missing, just like your case. Her body turned up a few days later in one of those shepherd huts scattered about the mountain.

"The police thought she had got lost, sheltered and frozen to death. But apparently the pathologist said she had been dead for three days, yet she had been spotted in the resort two days before her body was found.

"The police were baffled and I don't believe they ever solved the case."

"Which ski resort did this happen in?" asked Rose, suspecting she knew the answer.

"I think it was Val d'Isère. It was certainly one of the French resorts, which had an amazing seafood restaurant. I was served a whole crab on a silver platter and was given a pair of seafood crackers, like a nutcracker, to break the claws, and metal picks to delve out the meat.

"But I nearly ate the poisonous part of the crab without realising. I remember that. What a fun night, although it seemed strange to be eating seafood in the mountains, surrounded by snow and so far away from the sea."

"I wonder," muttered Rose to herself.

CHAPTER FORTY-EIGHT

Rose and Chris left the Cottage Hospital as lunch was being served. Chris drove Rose to Cape Chestnut restaurant, but he didn't stay. Rose hadn't arranged to meet anyone, but she didn't feel like being alone at home. She was unsettled and felt she needed to remain close to Craig, and the hospital.

She sat at the same small wooden table that she and Chris had occupied the previous Sunday, under the shade of the large Cape chestnut tree. As she ordered a passion fruit juice, her phone rang. She snatched it from the table, panicking that the hospital was calling about Craig, and answered briskly, "Hello".

"Rose, it's Chloe. I wondered if we could meet up. I'll buy you lunch."

"That's very kind," answered Rose, slightly breathlessly. "I've just arrived at Cape Chestnut. But you're welcome to join me."

"I'll come straight over."

Rose finished the call and thought about Chris's story and the dead woman on his skiing trip. Val d'Isère was the same place Robert had mentioned the previous evening. And he'd told them he and Vivian had both been there three years ago.

Was it just a coincidence? She wouldn't be at all surprised if Robert was the reason for his wife's disappearance. But had he killed her? If so, how? And did it mean he was responsible for other deaths, such as the poor woman in the ski resort?

And what about Vivian? She had appeared very uncomfortable when Robert mentioned Val d'Isère. But was that because 'bumping into each other' was just a phrase to cover up the fact that she and Robert had been staying at the resort together?

Rose's drink arrived. "Would you like to order food?" the waiter asked.

"Not yet, asante. I'm waiting for a friend."

He returned to the main restaurant building and as Rose removed her straw and sipped her passion fruit juice, she considered Vivian.

She had initially seen her at Nanyuki airstrip, the same day that she had first encountered the Scott Watsons. And at the marathon she thought she kept seeing the same woman, one with glossy brunette hair, flitting just out of view. Had that been Vivian?

Chloe had remarked that Vivian's surname, Scott, was similar to Robert's double-barrelled Scott Watson. Was that significant?

"Cooee," called Chloe, but with less than her usual enthusiasm.

A waiter followed her to the table and asked, "Would you like a drink?"

"Definitely. A gin and tonic, please. I better not make it a double though, as I am driving." Chloe flopped onto the chair opposite

Rose and exclaimed, "What a morning. How is Craig?"

How was Craig? Something was niggling at Rose about him this morning. To Chloe she said, "I think he's OK, but …"

"You're concerned something's wrong?" Chloe hung a small black leather bag on the back of her chair.

Rose swirled her drink with her straw. "I am, but nobody at the hospital seemed particularly concerned. I think I'm just being paranoid.

Perhaps puzzling over what happened to poor Nina Scott Watson is unsettling me. Do you know, Chris told me a strange tale today." Rose repeated Chris's story.

"Oh, international intrigue. Robert must be quite the lady's man." A hint of colour returned to Chloe's cheeks.

"You should have seen the way he was eyeing you up last night at supper. It seriously put Vivian's nose out of joint."

"Oh, so you also think they're friends with benefits." Chloe's drink arrived, and she took an appreciative sip.

"What do you mean by friends with benefits?" The phrase was new to Rose, although she thought she understood its meaning.

"You know, sometimes it's a little more than friends and they end up in the same bed." Now the whole of Chloe's face turned pink.

Rose leaned back in her wooden chair and said, "Yes, that's exactly what I think, and perhaps more than that. Just before you came, I was toying with your observation that both Robert and Vivian have Scott in their surnames."

Chloe leaned forward across the table and asked, "Do you believe they're related? Oh," Chloe cried, "Or were they married?"

"It's worth considering. And I don't think Nina was Robert's first wife, or second if he was actually married to Vivian." Rose tapped the side of her glass.

"So what are you going to do?" Chloe's eyes shone.

Rose sat up and sipped her fruit juice as she considered what to do next. "There's not much I can do, but perhaps Commissioner Akida can do some digging." She picked her phone up, tapped some keys and waited for the commissioner to answer.

He did, although he sounded distracted as he answered, "Mama Rose. I wasn't expecting to hear from you."

"I've been thinking …" responded Rose.

"Excellent," cut in the commissioner. "And do you know who killed Nina Scott Watson?"

"Not yet, but I wondered if you could look into something for me? Something relevant to the case. Do you have any contacts in the UK who could search for information about marriages?"

"I do, as a matter of fact," replied the commissioner. "And he owes me a favour. Tell me who you would like to look up."

"Well, firstly, can you find out if Robert Scott Watson has been married before, during the past twelve to fifteen years?"

"Ah, so you do think he did it. Constable Wachira told me Thabiti is convinced Robert Scott Watson killed his wife, but none of us can work out how."

"I'm still not sure. The pieces don't fit together at the moment. So, secondly, can your contact check if there has ever been a marriage between a Robert Scott and a Vivian someone? I'm afraid I don't have a surname.

"For that one we may need to look further back, up to say twenty years. And if he can't find anything in the UK, then, and this might be more difficult, but if it's possible, could he confirm if there is any record in the Philippines?"

"The Philippines? What have they got to do with it?" The commissioner sounded bemused.

"Probably nothing, but I'm just tying up loose ends."

"I'm not sure my favour extends that far, but I will try. Is there anything else? Is Bwana Craig well?"

"He's comfortable for the moment, and no, there's nothing else." Rose ended the call and as the waiter approached again she suggested, "Shall we check the menu board?"

She and Chloe approached the single-storey wooden restaurant building. The day's dishes were written on a large blackboard leaning against the wall on the veranda.

"Just the soup for me, tafadhali," Rose said to the hovering waiter.

"And I'd like the chicken salad."

Chloe and Rose returned to their table.

Rose hesitated before asking, "How was your session with the counsellor? Did you persuade Dan to accompany you?"

Chloe took another sip of her gin and tonic and replied, "Dan did come with me. He was conciliatory this morning and readily agreed. But I think he believed he was just supporting me. He became very defensive when the counsellor started probing him.

"He said things like, 'These are my red lines and I'm not crossing them'. And after the session he insisted on walking back and wouldn't get in the car with me." Chloe looked down at her hands and twisted her engagement ring.

Rose made her voice sound bright and positive as she said, "At least it's a step in the right direction. I guess he needs some time to himself to digest what you discussed." Rose leaned forward and placed her hand on Chloe's arm. "Don't push him too much over the next few days. When does he have to return to work?"

Chloe looked up at her. "Not until next Monday. They've postponed his return. And we've actually booked another session on Thursday. But I guess I'll just have to wait and see if Dan will come back with me."

Chloe opened her black bag and removed a lipstick and vanity mirror. A folded piece of paper drifted to the floor. As Chloe applied her lipstick, Rose picked up the paper which she recognised as a results sheet from the Lewa Marathon. Removing her glasses from her own tote bag, she skimmed through the names and times again.

Chris really had run very well, especially considering that he hadn't had long to adjust to the increase in altitude. And Chloe had done amazingly, even though her husband had been so dismissive.

Chloe replaced her lipstick and mirror in her bag and commented, "Dan gave me that today. He actually congratulated me, although I think he still resents that I ran so well."

"And you didn't have the support of teammates as he did. You ran and finished on your own."

Chloe bit at her freshly painted lips. "That's what I thought. But the result sheet shows that I didn't finish alone. In fact, and I really don't remember this, but perhaps she caught up with me when I fell. You see, Vivian Scott finished with me. With exactly the same time."

Rose leant back, rubbing her chin. She knew that couldn't be right. She had cheered poor Chloe home after she had fallen on the bend.

Her thoughts were interrupted as her phone rang. "Hello."

She sat up straight as the voice on the phone said, "Mrs Hardie. This is the Cottage Hospital. It's about your husband."

CHAPTER FORTY-NINE

Rose hastily climbed the concrete steps to the main entrance of the Cottage Hospital. She stopped and turned as Chris ran up behind her, taking the steps two at a time.

"Thanks for the call," he told his mother as they entered the main building.

Rose headed straight for the reception counter and said, before the receptionist could look up, "I've just had a call, about my husband, Craig. Craig Hardie."

"Rose," called Dr Farrukh from the entrance to the far corridor.

Rose and Chris dashed over to her.

"Follow me," she instructed and turned down the corridor, walking at a brisk pace. Rose tried, but failed, to keep up with Chris and the doctor as their route took them straight through and out of the building.

They turned left and entered a smaller, single-storey building with numerous closed doors leading from the central corridor. There was a stillness about the place and two nurses, standing further along the corridor, spoke to each other in hushed tones.

Chris and Dr Farrukh stopped by one of the doors and waited for Rose. Dr Farrukh whispered, "As I was telling your son, Craig has suffered a stroke and was unconscious when I last saw him." She opened the door and Rose stepped inside.

She felt as if she had stepped into an alien world. Craig was hooked up to monitors, and a see-though ventilator mask was strapped to his face and attached to a mechanical ventilation unit. A thin tube ran from his exposed ghostly-white hand to a bag of what must be IV fluid hanging from a stand.

Dr Farrukh and Chris followed her into the room and moved to the opposite side of the bed.

"What happened?" asked Rose hoarsely.

"The orderly who was giving him lunch noticed that Craig was slurring his words and that the left-hand side of his face had begun to droop. It was lucky he was there as he immediately pressed the emergency button."

Rose shook her head. "I knew something was wrong this morning. He just didn't seem himself and he said the pain was less than it had been but that he felt rather numb."

"Ah yes," interjected Dr Farrukh. "That is an early sign, but you weren't to know it would lead to a stroke. He could just have been feeling numb from lying in bed for a couple of days."

Chris turned and stepped towards the window. The view was obscured by white net curtains.

With his back to the room, Chris said, "Mum, I'm sorry I dismissed your concerns. It's like the doctor said, I just thought he was feeling the effects of lying down for a prolonged period." He bowed his head, "And I was irritated that you were late after spending the night at Borana."

Rose walked over to the window and placed a hand on her son's shoulder. "It's OK. We didn't know this would happen. Although, let's face it, we were all worried that he might take a turn for the worse."

Dr Farrukh picked up a chart, which she read. "And you did tell the nurse who checked on him this morning. It's written on here."

Rose went to stand by the doctor as she asked, "What are his chances of recovery?"

"I don't know. Let me try a few tests."

Chris left the window and stood by his father's bed opposite Rose and Dr Farrukh.

"Open your eyes," the doctor instructed her unconscious patient. There was no response. She repeated the question.

Dr Farrukh leaned over the bed and picked up Craig's frail hand, the one without the IV drip, and said, "Squeeze my finger."

Rose watched, feeling her arms tingle and silently thought, come on Craig. Just a little squeeze, just something to show you're still here with us.

Dr Farrukh repeated her command and Rose's eyes widened. She was certain she'd seen his fingers move. She looked up at the doctor, holding her breath.

The doctor stood up and smiled, "Good, there was some movement, so I think he will regain consciousness. Although we have no idea what damage has been done. I must check on another patient, but I'll be back shortly."

Rose and Chris sat facing the end of the bed in silence. Rose was not sure how long they stayed like that: it could have been two, five or twenty minutes.

A nurse entered the room and leant over Craig. "How are we doing, Mr Hardie?" After a pause she said calmly, "Oh good, you're awake. Just a minute whilst I remove your mask."

Rose and Chris both jumped up to stand beside Craig's bed. Rose clasped Craig's hand. The nurse unstrapped the ventilator mask and Craig turned his head just enough to smile at

Rose. She felt giddy and Chris grabbed her as her legs gave way. He helped her back to the chair where she sat for several minutes with her head between her legs.

She heard Chris say, "Don't worry, Dad. We're here. No, don't try to speak. Just rest and give yourself some time to recover."

Rose lifted her head and leant back in her chair. For the first time she noticed a warm glow permeate through the net covered window. The room seemed full of light ... and noise. Her mobile phone was ringing.

She answered it.

"Mama Rose." Commissioner Akida sounded excited.

"Just a minute, Commissioner." She stood up gingerly, but her legs bore her weight and as she walked across to the door she felt stronger. Outside Craig's room she said, "Sorry, please go on."

"You were right," he congratulated her. "My contact in the UK found records of Robert Scott Watson being married three times in the past twelve years, and that's in addition to his marriage to Nina. On two occasions his wives died, and the third went missing and was never found."

"Oh dear," murmured Rose as she leant against the corridor wall. "It's as I feared."

"My contact hasn't found any evidence of a marriage between a Robert Scott and a Vivian. He sent an email to the Philippines, but it's already seven in the evening there so he's not expecting a response until tomorrow morning at the earliest. What do you suggest we do now?"

Now. How could she think about what anyone else should be doing? Not when Craig was lying next door surrounded by all those machines.

"Mama Rose," she heard the commissioner call into the phone.

"Sorry." She massaged her temple. "Robert's wives," she said out loud.

"What about them?"

She willed her mind to think clearly. Money. Death. Into the phone she said, "Can one of your officers do some research into the wives?

How and where they died or went missing. Were they wealthy, and if so, did Robert inherit? And is there anything which is similar about the women or links them in any way?"

"Good idea. I'll get someone onto that straight away and I'll call you back with the results."

CHAPTER FIFTY

R ose pushed the phone into her pocket and followed Dr Farrukh back into Craig's room.

"Well done, Craig. You must have the constitution of a buffalo." Dr Farrukh examined the machines monitoring Craig. "Great, your vitals are returning to normal, but we don't want your blood pressure rising too high."

Craig opened his mouth, but only a hiss of sound came out. The doctor placed her hand on his arm. Don't try to speak just yet. It's going to take you time to recover and I don't want you getting worried and worked up. Just lean back and rest."

She turned to Rose and Chris and said, "I'll check back in an hour or so, but if you need me or a nurse, just press the red emergency button above the bed."

"Thank you, Doctor," Rose said as she felt her phone vibrate again in her pocket.

"What's going on, Mum? Why all the calls?" asked Chris.

She removed the phone and looked at the caller ID. "It's the commissioner again. He's got people looking up information which could solve the death of Nina Scott Watson."

Craig made another hissing sound, and they turned towards him. His eyes were wide and insistent.

Rose squeezed his hand. "It's OK. I'm just providing guidance, but I better take this call."

"Yes, Commissioner," Rose said as she answered the phone.

"Our enquiries have set some alarm bells ringing in the UK. I've just received a call from Thames Valley Police. It appears they're also interested in Robert Scott Watson. They've been tracking him for several years, but they hadn't found any evidence to implicate him in the deaths or disappearance of his wives. So they were most interested to hear his current wife has turned up dead in Kenya."

"Oh, I suppose they would be," Rose said self-consciously, feeling Chris's eyes upon her.

"And there's more. Again, you were right to suggest we look into the wives as they were all heiresses. The first was an older lady, a widow, but the others, including Nina, have been younger women with their own fortunes or sizeable trust funds.

"Thames Valley Police had already checked out Nina Scott Watson and found she'd changed her will before leaving for Kenya. And it will come as no surprise that Robert is the sole beneficiary."

"So you think Robert killed her?" Rose enquired.

"I do, but the trouble is we still don't know how. Do you?"

Did she? Pieces had been starting to fit together when she'd been sitting with Chloe at Cape Chestnut, but now her mind was heavy and she couldn't even fully process the information the commissioner had given her. When she had been at Cape Chestnut what had she considered needed doing? The enquiry into Robert and his marriages ... and to chat with Sam. But she couldn't remember why.

"I need to speak to Sam."

"Excellent. I'll pick you up and drive you across to Borana. Where are you? Home or at the hospital? And how is Craig?"

"Commissioner, he's not well. The doctors said he suffered a major stroke, and he's hooked up to all these machines."

"I am sorry. Is he awake? And stable?"

"Yes, for the moment."

"Then he's in the best place and there's not much you can do for him. If we leave now, we should be back by nightfall. But if we delay for too long, we risk Robert disappearing."

"I know, but ..."

"I'll be with you in ten minutes."

The phone went dead, but she continued to stare into it.

"You are not going anywhere," ordered Chris. "Not at the moment. Your place is by Dad's side."

Rose dropped her arms to her side as she said, "I know, and you're right. But I can't stand by and allow a man to escape. A man who almost certainly killed his wife, and probably several others, and who is likely to go on and kill again."

Chris stiffened his stance and argued, "Just leave it to the police. That's their job."

"I know, I know." Rose wrung her hands. "But they can't prove he did kill his wife. Nobody can at the moment. But I'm certain I was close to the truth earlier. I have to speak to Sam and have some space to think. I'm sure I can piece together what happened."

Chris's voice rose an octave. "But it's still not your job. Your role is as Dad's wife and you have a duty to be here with him. He needs you."

Rose felt an unaccustomed flash of anger and retorted, "My role. My duty. I've been by your father's side for over forty years and supported him through thick and thin. Who do you think provides food for our table since he retired? Me and my veterinary work. And what about your role? You're his only son, so you stay by his bed. Besides, what can either of us really do for him at the moment? He's getting all the medical care the hospital can provide and now he needs rest, and some peace to recover."

There was a hissing noise from the bed again. Rose felt stunned by her outburst, and Chris's mouth hung open.

"Go," whispered Craig.

"What was that, Dad?" Chris stammered.

Craig held eye contact with Rose and repeated a little stronger, "Go."

"I love you," said Rose as she pecked Craig on the cheek.

Her lips were wet, and she noticed tears trickling from his eyes.

"Goodbye," she whispered.

CHAPTER FIFTY-ONE

Commissioner Akida appeared to be a man possessed as he drove from Nanyuki to Borana. Speeding through the Ngara Ndare forest, he completely ignored the broken-up road and Rose clung to the grab handles as she was thrown from one side to another in the long wheelbase Land Cruiser, with its unforgiving suspension.

She felt sorry for the poor constable in the back of the vehicle and thought she heard him call out several times. She imagined him clinging to one of the wooden benches, but at least he would be protected from the worst of the dust the car was throwing up by the canvas cover.

Commissioner Akida must be confident of arresting Robert since he had brought this vehicle and the extra policeman.

At Aureus Lodge, she climbed out of the car, but placed a hand against it to steady herself. Sam and Constable Wachira approached.

"Ah, Constable," called the commissioner. "Perhaps we could run through some details while Mama Rose discusses what she needs to with Sam."

The commissioner walked towards the lodge and Sam looked expectantly at Rose with large enquiring eyes.

"I can't think," Rose said and shook her head in exasperation.

"Come, let's take a walk," Sam suggested. He gently took her arm as she weakly trod the first few steps. Her strength returned and she followed Sam along a winding path marked with white painted stones. They emerged at a bench placed under the shade of a cedar tree, overlooking Borana Conservancy and the Mathews range.

Sam indicated towards the bench. "Let's sit here while you gather your thoughts."

As Rose stared out at the vast expanse of wilderness, she felt awed by its permanence.

There was a discrete cough behind them and a member of staff placed a basket next to Sam and disappeared back down the track.

Sam chuckled as he removed a tin of Tusker. "And for you, a flask of what I'm guessing is tea."

He unscrewed the top and Rose watched the steam rise and smelt the sweet aroma. Bliss, she thought, leaning back on the bench, sipping her tea and gazing out at the landscape. Craig would love this. And she didn't feel either sorry or guilty. Instead she had the sensation of being whole, and that she was viewing the scene for both of them.

This is where Craig had felt most at home. Out in the bush. Not strapped to machines in a hospital ward. She understood now. His body was failing him, so he wanted to free his spirit and allow it to roam across the Kenyan savannah.

She felt a strong hand grip hers and turned to Sam with tears in her eyes. She whispered, "Thank you."

After several more minutes of silence, Sam said in a soft tone, "I believe you wanted to speak to me."

Rose took a deep breath. It was time to get to the bottom of this case, one way or another, so she could return to Nanyuki, to Craig. Her tote bag was on the bench beside her, and she reached in and extracted the piece of paper Chloe had dropped.

She unfolded it and handed it to Sam, "This is the results sheet from the Lewa Half Marathon. If you look a third of the way down the first side, you will see Chloe's name and time. And below it the name Vivian Scott with exactly the same time."

He stared at the sheet and queried, "You mean the Vivian Scott who is staying here at the lodge?"

Rose raised her eyebrows and replied, "I presume so. I don't think I can cope with anyone else named Scott."

"But I didn't know she ran at Lewa. Did Chloe recognise her in Nanyuki?"

Rose thought back and said, "I believe she did, but not from the race. She thought Vivian was the lady who'd joined her at Kongoni's swimming pool on Sunday morning, although Vivian was rather dismissive when she mentioned it."

"That is strange. Surely they would have congratulated each other if they'd finished the marathon together."

Rose turned to Sam and declared, "But they didn't."

"Didn't what?"

Rose tapped her thigh. "They didn't finish the race together. Chloe sped up around the final bend and slipped over. She picked herself up and ran gingerly to the finishing line, but she was on her own. I watched her."

"So how come Vivian Scott has the same finishing time?" Sam's eyes narrowed.

Rose looked down at her hands. "That's what I wanted to ask you."

Sam leaned back and looked out into Borana.
He began, "Thabiti was asking me about the equipment and running times the other day. You see, everyone's time begins the moment the starter shouts 'Go', even the competitors at the rear of the pack. And the only place where a time is registered is at the finishing line.

"We use transponder chips, which are attached to the back of the competitors' numbers, and monitoring equipment records their finishing time."

Rose rubbed her chin whilst she considered this information and finally commented, "So Vivian's transponder chip did cross the finish line at the same time as Chloe. Could someone have thrown it?"

Sam shook his head. "No, the monitoring equipment wouldn't have time to register it if it was thrown."

"So Chloe must have had the chip. She wouldn't have been carrying it in her hand, and if someone had attached it to her clothing surely she, an official, or another runner would have spotted it?"

"The most secure place would be on the back of her number with her own transponder chip. She would be unlikely to check there, and even if she did, she wouldn't know she had an extra chip. Perhaps we should call her and see if she still has her number, and if so, ask her how many chips are attached to the back."

Rose groaned. "Of course. Someone stole her number when she was having a massage after she finished the marathon."

"They must have been removing the incriminating evidence."

Rose looked out over Borana and said, "And I kept seeing someone, a woman very much like Vivian, out of the corner of my eye. At the start. At the water stop, where someone barged into Chloe. And again at the finish. Now I think about it, I believe she was deliberately trying to keep out of sight."

CHAPTER FIFTY-TWO

As Rose returned to the lodge with Sam along the winding path, she watched Commissioner Akida pacing up and down.

As soon as he spotted them, he rushed forward and asked, "So? Can we arrest Robert Scott Watson? Have you worked out how he killed his wife?"

Rose hesitated. "Not exactly, but I fear that by the time I have every piece of the puzzle he will realise we suspect him and abscond. I'll have to see if he implicates himself, or if Vivian does."

"So you think they were both responsible?" The commissioner clasped his hands together.

"Someone had to help Robert, as I don't see how he could have done it on his own. And Vivian is the most likely candidate. I would like to hear back from the Philippines, but as you said, it is night there, so we won't get a response until at least the morning."

Sam stepped forward and asked, "Where are Robert and Vivian at the moment?"

The commissioner looked at him and replied, "Marina told me they are together at the pool."

Sam seemed to consider his answer before stating, "Then I'll take the constable you brought with you, and station him behind the changing room to prevent our suspects escaping in that direction."

Sam turned and strode back to the commissioner's police vehicle.

"Shall we?" the commissioner asked Rose as he gestured towards the lodge entrance with his arm.

Rose took a deep breath and stepped inside.

Thabiti and Constable Wachira must have been watching out for them. They emerged from the drawing room and followed Rose and the commissioner.

The group bumped into Marina outside the dining room. "Are you going …?"

"Yes," interrupted Thabiti, and Marina joined Rose's entourage. They followed a path between the two main lodge buildings and entered the swimming pool area through a gap in the surrounding stone wall.

Vivian was lying on a sun lounger. She lifted her head, shielding her eyes with the magazine she had been reading, and exclaimed, "Are you all coming for a swim?"

Robert strode towards the bar and declared, "I think it's time for a drink. But I'll fix it myself as you're not much of a barman, Thabiti. You see, the secret of a perfect gin and tonic is to start with stemless wine glasses like these."

Robert picked up two rounded-bottom glasses and poured ice into them. "Half-fill them with ice and squeeze the juice from half a lime over the ice in each glass." Robert looked earnestly at Thabiti as he instructed, "The key is lime and not lemon juice." He walked behind the bar and started examining bottles of gin.

Constable Wachira tugged at Marina's arm and the two of them sat at the table, with shade provided by a large canvas umbrella, just beyond the entrance to the pool area. Thabiti sat on the wall by the entrance, but Rose and Commissioner Akida remained standing.

Robert picked up a bottle of Tanqueray gin and as he poured out measures, he continued, "Use a good quality gin and pour sixty millilitres into each glass. Unfortunately, you don't have any decent tonic, but never mind, I'll just add a splash of your sweet local tonic and fill the glass up with soda water. There we are, just a slice of lime to garnish."

He lifted the two full glasses in triumph and walked towards Vivian. He handed her a glass as he sat on the second sun lounger.

"Cheers," he said, clinking glasses with Vivian. He took an appreciative sip and then looked up at Rose and Commissioner Akida.

Constable Wachira brought a chair for Rose, but the Commissioner remained standing.

Rose actually felt strengthened by Robert's discourteous behaviour. Irritated by his arrogance, she remarked in a frosty tone, "I suppose you've shared many gin and tonics together. In glamorous locations. And since you arrived in Nanyuki, Robert."

She turned to face Vivian. "You've always been close by, haven't you Vivian? Or should I say Mrs Scott? You are Mrs Scott, aren't you? Robert's first and only legal wife."

Robert leaned forward and whispered to Vivian, "You don't need to say anything, darling."

Vivian smiled at him. A large smile like that of the famed Cheshire cat in Alice in Wonderland. "Oh, I think you've rather given the game away. It's been fun, but it was bound to end sooner or later. And I did tell you to leave poor little Nina alone, but you insisted on marrying the stupid girl."

This was going better than Rose had expected. She decided to throw an imaginary dart into the dark and stated, with more confidence than she felt, "You were married in the Philippines all those years ago. So what happened?"

Vivian sat up and sighed. "I was young and naive, and he swept me off my feet. We had some fun times together, but it didn't take me long to realise the kind of man Robert is. He would never stay faithful to just one woman."

"Darling," Robert drawled.

Vivian ignored him.

Bullseye, thought Rose. She was right, they had been married in the Philippines, and she remembered the crossword clue Chris had read out to Craig in the hospital. "But divorce is illegal in the Philippines."

"Yes, there and the Vatican City," Vivian agreed. "One of only two places in the whole world, so I was tied to Robert."

She looked back at him, as a mother might with a wayward child. "So my father suggested I go away for a while, and he found me a job on a yacht sailing around the Mediterranean. By the time I returned home, he had packed Robert off back to London."

She swirled the remaining ice in her glass, and continued, "I learnt later that Robert hadn't been keen on finding another job, and without a reference from my father, I doubt anyone would have employed him. So instead he found and charmed a wealthy middle-aged widow. But there was one condition on his marrying her, that Robert took her name, which he did by adding it to his own. Very clever really, and I would have been none the wiser if I hadn't bumped into them a couple of years later in Venice."

Vivian stood and moved across to sit next to Robert. She laid her free hand on his leg and with a lopsided smile remarked, "But you didn't like being treated like a lackey, did you? Or a gigolo for her friends to fawn over?"

Robert met Vivian's gaze and shook his head. "She really was an awful woman. And she treated me like her lap dog, always commanding me to 'Fetch this' or 'Get that.'

"And then there was her constant social climbing with its relentless instruction. 'If you want to mix with Dukes and Countesses, you have to learn the right words. Always say "loo" or "lavatory" but never "toilet" or "bathroom", and it's a "sofa" not a "settee". She even made me change the way I laughed as she said I brayed like a donkey. She quite drove me to distraction."

Vivian patted his leg, "But she did refine your social skills, and she taught you how to make these wonderful gin and tonics."

They both raised and clinked their glasses together again as Rose wondered if they were recalling past events.

CHAPTER FIFTY-THREE

Rose felt hot and uncomfortable sitting beside the swimming pool at Aureus Lodge, even though the intensity of the sun was waning in the late afternoon. Robert Scott Watson and Vivian Scott sat side by side on a sun lounger, their eyes locked together.

Thabiti jumped off the wall where he had been sitting, and dragged a large canvas umbrella across to shade Rose and the still, upright figure of Commissioner Akida.

Marina left in the direction of the main lodge building.

Rose coughed and asked Robert and Vivian, "So what did you do about Robert's over-bearing wife?"

Robert answered, "I realised my mistake and that I still loved Vivian. I made up my mind to divorce Donna, that was her name, so we could be together again."

Vivian turned to face Rose, shrugged her shoulders, and divulged, "But Robert had given up his job and wasn't interested in finding another. And I had no qualifications, nor had I any intention of doing any proper work."

Robert took up the story, "And in my haste to be married I hadn't realised I was signing a prenuptial, and that all Donna's money was tied up in a trust. If I divorced her, I would only get a measly £10,000."

"So you killed her?" queried Rose.

Robert crossed his arms. "So she died, and we walked away with her money and were happy."

"For a time," conceded Vivian. "But then you started to take an active interest in the pretty girls we met on our travels. And you were fed up with always being on the move and wanted us to return to England. But I had no intention of going there. I wanted to travel to America."

Vivian rested her hands behind her on the sun lounger and leaned back. "So, you left for London, where you wooed and married a dull girl from Berkshire, and I tried my luck on the silver screen."

"But you weren't very successful," quipped Robert.

Vivian appeared to ignore his biting tone and responded dryly, "I was too old by then to make any meaningful impact. But it was fun, and I was given a couple of walk on parts. But you were soon pestering me again and complaining about Stella. You both flew over to the States to visit me and, whoops, she had a boating accident and died." Vivian raised her eyes to the sky.

Rose pressed on and asked, "And what about Val d'Isère?"

"Oh, you are clever," Vivian said in a patronising tone. "That was sweet little Felicity, although she did annoy me with her constant giggling. I was sorry to get rid of her, and that should have been the end of it."

She sat up and turned to Robert. "But you went and met Nina at Royal Ascot, when I was back in the States, and the game began again. You swore she'd be the last, and I guess now she will be."

"Not if I can help it." Robert dashed to the wall, placed his hands on the top and sprung over it. He turned to the left, but the young police constable stepped out onto the path. Robert turned and sped in the opposite direction.

Vivian stood and clapped. She shouted, "Oh, bravo," as Robert disappeared around the corner.

He returned a few moments later in the clutches of Sam.

"Good try," called Vivian.

Marina and the lodge staff arrived with trays of sandwiches and cake, and one of the staff carried two thermos flasks.

"I think we all need to cool down in the pool house," commanded the commissioner.

Sam held Robert whilst the constable handcuffed him and then led him across to the pool house, following the commissioner.

Vivian wrapped a striped kikoi around her waist and stuffed her magazine inside her bag. She placed her feet in a pair of beaded flip-flops and was escorted by Constable Wachira to the pool house.

Rose, Thabiti and Sam hung back.

"What a story," said Thabiti in an awestruck tone.

"But I'm not sure it really helps us," admitted Rose.

Sam tapped his fingers together. "Robert as good as admitted his guilt by trying to run away, but neither of them have said anything which will stand up in court."

Thabiti shuffled his feet. "But they admitted to killing those other women."

"Not exactly," Sam replied. "There were no details, and they could argue it was just a story they made up to amuse themselves and confuse us."

"Sam's right," agreed Rose. "We need details of how they committed this crime and for them to admit their guilt."

Rose bit her lip. "But I think I know how they did it, and if I'm right, I think one or the other will cave in. Probably Vivian. I believe she always thought this last venture was a folly, and I suspect she's tired of travelling around the world bumping off women whenever Robert gets tired of them."

"It's worth a try," agreed Sam. "Especially as I doubt any additional evidence will come to light now. The only risk is that they walk free, which it looks like they would do anyway."

Rose squared her shoulders and marched toward the pool house, flanked by Sam and Thabiti.

CHAPTER FIFTY-FOUR

Rose walked into the pool house and took the proffered cup of tea from Marina, but remained standing by the table. Thabiti piled sandwiches and cakes onto a plate and joined Sam, who was leaning against the far wall.

In a semi-circle, facing Rose, were Vivian and Constable Wachira, sitting on a large wooden sofa, Commissioner Akida in a large armchair, and Marina on a wooden safari chair, nearest the entrance to the pool house.

The constable still held onto Robert and they stood behind the commissioner, far from the entrance to the building.

They all looked expectantly at Rose.

She cleared her throat and began, "By now we know that you killed your wife, although legally, I'm not sure she was your wife. Anyway, you killed Nina with Vivian's help, but how you did it has puzzled all of us. So let's start with when.

"All along we've believed that the last reported sightings were on Sunday morning, when Nina was seen walking alone into Borana Conservancy, from where she disappeared. But that wasn't Nina, was it? That was you, Vivian?"

Vivian opened her arms wide, "But I'd never visited the lodge until I drove here with you and your friend yesterday."

"Then how did you know the name of the artist who painted the jackal picture? It's only just been mounted on the dining room wall."

The commissioner's eyes widened in surprise.

"And I haven't had a chance to post about it on social media," added Marina.

Vivian looked down at her lap and pulled at a thread of her kikoi wrap.

Rose addressed her. "Nina didn't return to the lodge after the Lewa Marathon, did she? You came in her place, and when you heard us all arrive back, you made sure you kept out of sight in Robert's bedroom. You feigned tiredness and didn't join us for supper."

Vivian's mouth was pinched as she crossed her arms over her chest.

"The next morning you snuck out of the lodge early, wearing Nina's hat so that anyone who spotted you would think you were Nina. Did you deliberately walk past the yoga group to ensure you were seen?"

Vivian stared at Rose with hostile eyes and refused to answer.

"I believe you drove here on Friday night. I'm not sure where you got the car from, but you parked it in the whistling thorn bushes by the watering hole, where it was hidden from sight.

"Then you called the camp manager at Lewa, telling him you'd got lost taking a shortcut and that your car had broken down. He sent a man to pick you up, and you spent the night at Lewa ready for Saturday morning's marathon."

Rose's mouth was dry, so she took a sip of tea. Her audience waited in silence. "When I saw Nina at the marathon, I was surprised to see she was wearing a bright pink running vest. I understand it represents a breast cancer charity in the UK, and you used its distinctive colour to your advantage.

"After killing her, you wore her pink vest over your black top and from then on you impersonated Nina. At a designated spot on the marathon course, Robert lured Nina into the copse of white thorn acacia trees. I guess he suggested a loo stop away from prying eyes or something like that. Had you chosen the spot on your earlier visit to Lewa, Vivian?"

"What earlier visit?" interjected the commissioner.

Rose looked at him and explained, "When I first saw Vivian, at Nanyuki airstrip, she was disembarking from Safari Link's Lewa flight."

"I see," said the commissioner, nodding this head.

"One of you strangled her." Rose eyed the two suspects and then pronounced, "Vivian, was it you? After all, you appear to be the one with the brains and courage in this partnership. I'm not sure what you used and if it's a method you've perfected."

Vivian continued to stare at Rose with hard, cold eyes.

Rose shivered and said, "Initially it was impossible to say how Nina had been killed, as the marks on her neck only became apparent over time. And if her body had not been discovered by the tracker dogs, it is likely to have disappeared the way all corpses do in the wild. And then her death would never have come to light, and she would have remained a missing person."

Vivian tried to stand, but Constable Wachira grabbed her arm and pulled her back onto the wooden sofa.

Rose turned towards Robert, who was red in the face and snatching at his handcuffs. "But you still had one major obstacle. Whilst Vivian could effectively become Nina, by wearing her bright pink running vest and hiding her hair under a baseball cap, the race officials would know that two women started the race, but only one of them finished. They are very careful about competitors' safety, so they would have sent out a search party."

Sam asked from the back of the room, "But if she wore Nina's vest over her own, they would both be marked as finishing."

Rose looked over at Sam and nodded. "They would, but as we discussed earlier, both women would be given the same time. Now, I doubt anyone would have looked at Nina's finishing time, or cared that a Vivian Scott completed the marathon at exactly the same moment, but it was not a risk I believe Vivian was willing to take.

"I was standing by one of the water stops when someone pushed Chloe. Was that you, Vivian?" She turned back to Vivian, who was once again examining her kikoi wrap.

"Did you attach your transponder chip to Chloe's number? Chloe was also distinctive that day with her blonde hair and a baby blue and pink running top. And you probably noticed that she was fit and would finish the race before you and not be struggling along at the back."

"Why would that matter?" asked Marina.

"Because it would allow Vivian time to retrieve the transponder chip before she and Robert returned to the lodge ahead of us. Did Robert ask for a separate vehicle to collect them?"

"Yes, he did," admitted Marina.

"He needed to ensure their privacy on the journey so nobody would realise it was Vivian and not Nina returning," explained Rose.

"And was it Vivian who stole Chloe's number whilst she was having a massage?" Marina asked.

"Vivian or Robert, I'm not sure which. But Robert made sure we saw him, and also his wife, who was sitting on the floor, wrapped in a kikoi and wearing a hat."

"That's quite a story," said Vivian in a nonchalant tone as she tapped her fingertips together. "Almost as good as the one I told you. But there's no proof of anything you've told us."

"Perhaps not," said the commissioner, striding across to Rose's side. "But it is enough to arrest you both and throw you into a Kenyan prison. And I don't mean Nanyuki. I think the one at Isiolo might suit you better." His jaw tightened.

"Oh, that's grim," muttered Thabiti. "It's hardly been updated since it was built just after the Second World War. And didn't they recently have an outbreak of cholera?"

The colour drained from Vivian's suntanned face.

"They did," agreed the commissioner, swaying backward and forwards on the soles of his feet. "Ten inmates died this time. And it's going to be a long, drawn-out process, finding and interviewing everyone who took part in the marathon, or who was officiating. And then we need to find the car and track the owner and …"

"I'll call my lawyer," shouted Robert. "And make sure we're extradited to the UK."

"But we couldn't allow you to leave the country if we are still collecting evidence and need to interview you further," said the commissioner in a superior tone.

Robert blinked rapidly, as if taking in the seriousness of his position. "All right," he blurted. "We did kill Nina."

Vivian turned to him and hissed, "Be quiet. He's bluffing."

"Am I?" the commissioner asked as he raised his eyebrows.

"It's like the old lady said," Robert declared. "Vivian strangled Nina during the race and we left her body in some trees hoping the animals would destroy it. Then Vivian pretended to be Nina. She walked out on Sunday morning to the car she had hidden near the watering hole and drove back to Nanyuki."

CHAPTER FIFTY-FIVE

S am and Rose stood in the entrance of the pool house and watched Commissioner Akida as he charged Robert Scott Watson and Vivian Scott with the murder of Nina Scott Watson.

They stepped back to allow Marina and Thabiti past, carrying trays of sandwiches and cakes back to the lodge.

"Just a minute," called Sam, and he helped himself to several sandwiches.

Thabiti drew close to Rose and muttered, "I knew Robert killed his wife, but I just couldn't work out how he did it."

"And that was one of the issues. The crimes were committed in different locations, different countries even, making it almost impossible for the authorities to connect them. And it enabled Robert and Vivian to perfect their routine and keep repeating it. They killed all those poor women."

Marina and Thabiti walked towards the lodge, and Commissioner Akida joined Rose and Sam.

The commissioner rubbed his hands together and said, "Congratulations, Mama Rose. That's another case you've successfully solved. And if you hadn't, I doubt we would ever have learnt the truth. You are like a wise old chimpanzee, which watches what those around her are doing and draws conclusions from their actions. Don't you agree, Sam?"

"I do, and this time I was completely in the dark. It hadn't dawned on me that Nina never returned to the lodge after the race. Once you realised that, I suppose everything slipped into place."

"Not exactly," responded Rose. "I guessed what they had done, but I doubt we would have found any evidence, even if you did interview all the competitors and officials."

She turned to the commissioner and said, "By the way, that was an inspired move. Without it, and the threat of Isiolo prison, I think Vivian would have persuaded Robert to remain silent and we wouldn't have been able to prove they killed Nina."

The young constable approached them, escorting a still struggling Robert. As they walked past, Robert spat, "You meddling old witch. If it hadn't been for you, we would have got away with it."

Rose raised her eyebrows at Sam.

He laughed and said, "Don't take it personally."

Constable Wachira led Vivian by the arm. They stopped beside the commissioner, who said to Vivian, "We won't handcuff you if you behave and don't try to escape. The journey will be uncomfortable, and you'll need your hands to steady yourself. But if you try anything, anything at all, my constable will not hesitate to restrain you."

"Where are you taking us?" Vivian asked, in a dignified voice with just a quiver of anxiety.

The commissioner replied, "To the police station at Nanyuki. You will be formally charged and brought before the magistrate tomorrow, and either returned to the police station, for more questioning, or sent to Nanyuki prison to await trial."

Vivian looked out over Borana and up at the sky. Rose followed her gaze and watched a bird circling above them.

Vivian sighed. "Will I ever be free like that again?"

Constable Wachira led her away as Rose continued to watch the bird. It swooped down and perched on a yellow poui tree. It tilted its head. Was it watching her? Or trying to tell her something? And then it rose into the sky, flying above their heads so its white undercarriage and the red tip of its tail were clearly visible. It swooped over them again crying k'werk, k'werk, k'werk and then soared up and out over Borana.

"What a beautiful bird," mused Rose.

"An augur buzzard," noted Sam. "I wonder if it was searching for its mate, as they're often seen in pairs."

"A free spirit," said Commissioner Akida in an unusually emotional tone.

The mood was broken by a shout and the pounding of footsteps, and they turned as Thabiti ran towards them. Catching his breath, he said, "Mama Rose, it's Craig. The Cottage Hospital just called. He's had another stroke."

Rose looked up at the sky, but the buzzard had vanished. She felt a heaviness inside her chest. Life would never be the same without Craig.

"Come, Mama Rose. We must leave immediately for Nanyuki," urged the commissioner.

She felt a large arm encircle her shoulders, and she lent into Sam's reassuringly robust frame as he led her to the commissioner's car.

Marina was standing by the vehicle holding a brown paper bag. She hugged Rose and said, "Something for the journey, or later when you feel like eating."

"Do you want me to come with you?" Thabiti asked as he kicked at a stone in the dusty ground.

"Thank you, but there's no need," said Rose in a brittle voice. "Chris will be at the hospital."

She climbed into the commissioner's vehicle and as the car backed away, she watched Marina place her arm around Thabiti and wave them off.

CHAPTER FIFTY-SIX

An orderly escorted Rose to the room where she had left Craig and Chris earlier in the afternoon, but when she opened the door, the first person she saw was her daughter Heather.

Heather rushed forward and hugged her. When Heather finally released Rose, she cried, "Oh Mum, I'm so relieved to see you."

Bemused, Rose responded, "And me you, but when did you arrive?"

"This morning. I caught the overnight flight via Amsterdam, and then a taxi up to Nanyuki. I just missed you this afternoon."

Rose looked at the empty space where Craig's bed had been. Had she also missed him? Had he been taken away already?

"Where's your father?" she asked quietly. "Did you see him?"

Chris, who was sitting on one of the chairs opposite the empty space, answered softly, "They've taken Dad for a second CT scan."

Heather smiled weakly. "I did get to see him. And I told him all about the girls. He was struggling to speak, but he smiled and seemed happy for me to be here."

"I'm sure he was delighted." Rose felt a wave of relief. "Actually, I think he's been holding on to see you. But we weren't expecting you until the end of the month."

Heather rubbed her arm. "Chris has been keeping me updated and as soon as I heard about Dad's fall, I began making arrangements to fly over."

The door opened and Craig's bed was wheeled into the room, followed by Dr Farrukh. As Craig was being hooked up to various monitors and the drip, Dr Farrukh addressed them.

"I'm afraid it's as I feared." To Rose she said, "We undertook a CT scan of his brain immediately after his stroke and discovered that one of his arteries was blocked by a blood clot. We've been trying to dissolve it with medication delivered via his drip."

She stepped towards them with her lips drawn together and a look of sympathy in her eyes, "But it's not working. The second scan showed the clot is still there. The only option now is surgery to remove it, but it might not work, and his chances of surviving the procedure are low."

Chris asked, "What damage will the blood clot have already done?"

The doctor's tone was soft as she answered, "Considerable, I would expect. He was already struggling to speak after his last stroke, and this one is likely to have damaged his brain further."

"Can he breathe on his own, without all these machines?" asked Heather.

"No," replied the doctor, giving a small shake of the head.

Rose walked across to Craig's bed and took hold of his frail hand. It felt cold and as she looked at his closed eyes and expressionless face she whispered, "It's time to let him go."

Heather wrapped an arm around her shoulder and asked, "Are you sure?"

"But you didn't get a chance to say goodbye to him," Chris said with a sad, almost apologetic tone.

Without looking up, Rose whispered, "Yes. I did."

CHAPTER FIFTY-SEVEN

Wednesday morning was bright and sunny with a slight north-easterly wind. Rose tasted moisture on the air and hoped it signalled rain for Timau and the surrounding areas. Timau had always experienced a slightly different weather pattern from Nanyuki, and historically had its heaviest rainfall in July.

She remembered when Craig had been a farm manager near the town. As July approached, he would become increasingly agitated as he needed rain to replenish the soil with moisture, in readiness for August's planting season, but at the same time, he didn't want storms to flatten the ripening corn and peas on those areas of the farm which were awaiting harvest.

She entered Nanyuki's crematorium with Chris and Heather. It was a sombre place with concrete floors and crumbling walls, but at least it was open to the sky. A mound of firewood had been built in the centre and Craig's coffin rested on top of it.

Beside her, Heather gasped.

"Are you OK?" Chris asked his sister.

"Yes," she stammered. "It's just that I was expecting something more like the UK, where the body is cremated out of sight of the mourners. It's so ..."

"Explicit?"

"Yes, I guess so, but it's also definitive, and typically Kenyan. Keep it plain, simple and natural."

There were only the three of them staring at the funeral pyre. Rose had thought about asking close friends, but wasn't sure where to draw the line. Instead, they had decided on a small family only cremation followed by a scattering of ashes at Borana.

Rose had booked St George's Church for a memorial service on Saturday. Although she was Catholic, Craig had remained an Anglican. He had only attended church occasionally, but it had either been to St Georges's in Nanyuki, or The Church of the Good Shepherd in Timau.

A member of the hospital staff stepped forward. He wore a grey suit, which was fraying at the ends of the sleeves and had a hole in the arm. It looked like a burn mark as the edges were copper-coloured. He asked, "Are you ready? Shall we begin?"

Chris walked away with the man who lit and handed him a burning torch. Slowly and steadfastly, Chris approached the pyre and, holding the torch to the dry wood, ignited it. Rose watched and under her breath she mumbled,

"O God, Creator and Redeemer,
Of all Your faithful people,
Grant to the souls of all our faithful departed

Your mercy, light and peace.
Lord, we pray that those we love,
Who have gone before us in faith,
May know your forgiveness for their sins.
And the blessings of everlasting light,
In the company of the Virgin Mary,
And all the angels and saints in ancient Heaven.
Amen"

Beside her Heather wept, and after several minutes, she turned away from the flames. Rose watched small particles rise into the air where they were caught by a gust of wind and carried away. She said solemnly in Swahili. "Hakuna chanson kisicho na mwisho," and repeated in English, "There is no beginning that has no end. Everything has an end."

Chris put his arm around her and observed, "Heather's very upset. I suggest we go home and I'll return in a couple of hours to collect the ashes. Then we can drive out to Borana."

"I think that's best. When I spoke to Marina this morning, she told me Thabiti had left in search of the perfect spot to scatter your father's ashes. Somewhere the wind will carry them away across Laikipia, just as he wanted."

CHAPTER FIFTY-EIGHT

That afternoon, Rose stood on top of the escarpment, close to Aureus Lodge, in Borana Conservancy.

Chris held up a wine glass, filled with ash from the cremation, and toasted his father with a small speech. "Dad, we may have had our differences over the years, but I am grateful, and thankful, that we were reunited and we were able to spend some precious time together."

He paused and then continued, "Your life was not always easy, and from early childhood you fought to overcome adversity. I now realise that you only ever did what you thought was best for me, and for all of us. We have been flooded with cards and messages from your friends and colleagues, which have led me to understand how important and influential you were in so many different areas.

"In farming, you developed sustainable systems to grow crops on marginal tracts of land. You worked on the conservation, preservation and integration of wildlife within the community, and you served on many local committees, including the North Kenya Polo Club and the Mount Kenya Horse Show. You will be remembered for all the great work you did, and you will be sorely missed."

He raised his glass to the sky and then emptied it out over the escarpment. The ashes danced and swirled as they were caught by the gentle breeze.

Heather was next. In a strained voice, with tears running down her cheeks, she said, "Oh, Dad, I'll miss you so much. I wish I could have spent more time with you this year, but I have my family in the UK, and the girls are growing up so quickly. They loved their visits here and I remember when you taught them to fish and you all ended up in a reservoir. There was so much noise that I was worried someone had drowned. And there were the amazing game drives you took us on with sundowners at the rocks overlooking your beloved Laikipia. I can't believe you're gone."

She stopped and wiped her eyes with her sleeve. "Goodbye, Dad." She tipped her wine glass of ashes over the edge of the escarpment, turned back to Chris and buried her head in his chest.

He wrapped his arms around her and said in a soothing voice, "It's OK. It's good to grieve and not bottle it all up."

Rose stepped forward and surveyed the open savannah in front of her. She raised her eyes from the far off Mathew's range to the clear blue sky.

A bird circled above her and, as it came closer, she recognised the white undercarriage and the red tail of the augur buzzard. It k'werked at her several times before rising higher into the sky.

"I see you," she murmured. "You're free now, my love. No more pain, no more immobility, and no more reliance on other people. You can do, feel and see whatever you want. Watch over and protect us, and when I'm about to do something rash or stupid, please remind me to stop and think. We've had over forty wonderful years together, and even when life was hard, it really made us appreciate the good times."

She looked down at the ground and then back out into the savannah, and said, "I'll really miss you, especially at breakfast on our patio, when we'd watch the inquisitive red-cheeked cordon-bleu birds land on the stone bird table, under the bottlebrush tree, and peck at whatever offerings Kipto had left them.

And what shall I do with all your crossword puzzles? I'm not sure Thabiti will be as interested now you're not around to help him, and I've never really had the patience, or inclination to complete them."

She paused and smiled to herself. Heather was still wrapped in Chris's embrace. "Goodbye and safari salama." She stepped to the edge of the escarpment, raised her glass to the heavens and emptied it into the wind.

The remaining ashes from the cremation were contained in a wooden box. Chris walked further along the escarpment, placed the box on the ground and removed the lid.

Returning to Rose and Heather, he said, "The wind will gradually catch the ashes and bear them away."

They turned and walked back to the lodge.

CHAPTER FIFTY-NINE

T hat evening, Rose felt drained and empty as she entered the dining room at Aureus Lodge. She looked across at the painting of the jackals, which had helped her solve Nina Scott Watson's murder.

Marina, Thabiti, Pearl, Chris and Heather all stood behind their allocated dining chairs and waited. At the top end of the table, Thabiti picked up a pint glass of Tusker, looked nervously around the room and then down at the table as he said, "I would like to propose a toast to Craig."

The others waited in silence. "I didn't know him for long, but I can't thank him enough for being there and supporting me after Ma's death. Our regular crossword puzzle get-togethers became friendly sparring matches, but he always had the upper hand."

He raised his glass and everyone around the dining table followed his example, as they all chorused, "To Craig."

The lodge staff carried in starters of mushroom and parmesan tartlets.

Marina turned to Rose, and asked, "Will you stay at your house in Nanyuki?"

Rose spread pâté over a piece of toast and replied, "Yes, I think so, as long as I can keep paying the rent. I enjoyed living in the bush but at my age Nanyuki's far more convenient. Besides, I still have plenty of space for my animals."

Chris asked across the table. "What about the bills and the staff payroll? I remember Dad was always so meticulous with his paperwork."

"He was, but I've been taking a more active role. I've dealt with the staff wages for over a year, although I get irritated with the long queues at the NSSF office each month."

Thabiti finished his mouthful and added, "Craig showed me his files and talked me through the bills. I hope to be able set up some regular online payments which can be paid directly from Craig's pension."

Rose produced a lopsided smile and said, "In a way it was a relief Craig was not in hospital for long. Besides not extending his suffering, it also kept his hospital fees at a manageable level. There had been talk about him moving into the Louise Decker Centre, but I'm not sure how we could have paid for that."

"Mum," instructed Heather, "I don't want you to be short of money, and I know what you're like, you'll make sure your animals and staff are fed before you. So if you are ever in trouble, call me and either Chris or I will help you out. Won't we?" She turned to her brother.

"Of course," Chris nodded as he chewed a mouthful of toast and pâté. He swallowed and remarked, "In fact, I've been looking into setting up a regular payment plan so that there is a financial cushion should any of us need it."

Marina asked, "How long are you both staying in Nanyuki?"

Chris sipped his wine and answered, "I'll have to leave on Sunday, as I'm flying from Heathrow to Oman on Monday evening for a work contract. And I'll be away for a month."

Heather reached across the table and said, "I'll stay as along as you need, Mum, although I should try to get back next week if I can, for the girls, and work."

Marina looked across the table at Thabiti and proposed, "We can help next week, can't we?"

Thabiti nodded.

Marina continued in a regretful tone, "And since we've been asked to leave tomorrow, we can also help with the memorial service."

"Why so sudden?" asked Pearl. "All of my yoga group were really impressed with the lodge and how well you hosted us. In fact, I thought you'd be given the manager's position on a permanent basis. You've done such a great job here."

Marina tapped the table. "Apart from one of my guests being murdered, and two more being arrested for the crime. The owners are understandably upset, although they were the ones who offered the lodge to the Scott Watsons in the first place. Apparently, a new couple are arriving on Saturday for a management trial period, and they want Thabiti and I packed up and away tomorrow."

Thabiti raised his pint glass of Tusker towards Marina and stated, "So this is our last night. We'd better make the most of it."

He toasted Marina, who responded by raising her own glass of passion fruit juice.

Heather enquired, "So what are you both going to do next?"

Marina placed her knife and fork on her empty plate and replied, "I'm fed up of dealing with tourists and guests, especially ones who kill each other. I want to do something more meaningful, so I've arranged a meeting tomorrow morning with Stella MacDonald. You might know that she has a senior role with the charity Global Vista, and I might volunteer to work at one of their outreach camps."

Chris scratched his head. "That's not work for the faint-hearted. They have a base at Kakuma Refugee camp in Turkana County. We sometimes recruit from the camp or its neighbouring Kalobeyei settlement. I've visited, and it's pretty harrowing."

Marina leant forward. "But those are people who need help, and it's where I might be able to make a difference." She sat up. "Anyway, I'll see what Stella says tomorrow."

"And what about you, Thabiti?" asked Chris. "Will you go with Marina?"

Thabiti hesitated and looked at Pearl, "No, I don't think so."

Pearl remarked brightly, "Don't hold back on my account."

He turned to her and asked, "Why? What are you doing?"

"I'm going to India for a yoga and martial arts retreat."

Thabiti opened his eyes wide and exclaimed, "On your own?"

She laughed, "Yes, Thabiti, on my own. I am capable, you know. I've discussed it all with Dr Emma. Food and accommodation are provided at the retreat. And they've even arranged transport to collect me from the airport. And if I get really stuck, Dr Emma has some veterinary contacts in India who she's sure will help me."

Rose said in a confused tone, "Why is Dr Emma helping you?"

"Because she's taken over the management of our trust." Pearl bit into a piece of toast and pâté.

Thabiti turned to Rose, and explained, "I helped Craig sort it all out after we returned from the Rhino Charge. I guess he knew then that his time was limited."

"Good on you," Heather said to Pearl. "That sounds like a fascinating trip."

Chris laughed at Thabiti, who was rubbing his chin and looking perplexed. "So, you're going to be on your own."

"It seems that way," admitted Thabiti. "But it might give me a chance to explore hydroponics and permaculture. I've been really impressed with the permaculture system Borana has set up, but there has to be a way to combine it with hydroponics so food can be grown in harsher, drier environments, but without unsightly greenhouses."

Marina turned back to Rose. "And what are your plans for Craig's memorial service? I expect there will be quite a crowd."

"We're holding the service at St Georges Church in Nanyuki and the wake at Cape Chestnut. You'll both do a reading, won't you?"

She looked towards Heather and Chris who nodded. "And Craig's old polo chum Dickie Chambers is giving the eulogy. I'm trying to find out if the Moipei Sisters are in the country and if they'd be willing to come and sing. Craig and I so love their song, 'My Land is Kenya'."

Marina reached out and touched Rose's arm, and with tears in her eyes said, "So do I. And let me know if I can help."

CHAPTER SIXTY

Thabiti leaned against the wooden rail of the viewing platform outside the drawing room of Aureus Lodge.

Marina joined him, and as she stared out over Borana Conservancy, she said, "I'd swear it's become even drier since we arrived. The grass has turned brown and much of it has been eaten away by the wildlife."

"Kenneth, the gardener, believes they'll have some rain soon, so hopefully there'll be a new growth of grass. Have you finished packing?"

Marina turned back to the lodge and replied, "I think so. The staff have said that if we leave anything behind, they'll take it to Nanyuki and leave it at Dormans for me to collect. Have you enjoyed it here?"

Thabiti considered the question before answering. "It's been interesting, I'll give you that. And the lodge is amazing, but it's not really my thing. We were lucky to have mostly friends staying, as I really don't like groups of strangers, especially if they are rude or arrogant, and I have to be nice to them."

"Or when one of them kills another, and although you suspect what he's done, you have to carry on doing his bidding as you can't prove anything."

"Something like that," agreed Thabiti, still staring out at the conservancy. "But the sense of space out here, and absence of human interference, it both fascinates and scares me. I don't think I could live out in the bush. I've realised that although I struggle to deal with people, I do need to be around them, and in some small way, connected to them." He turned around and looked into the lodge. "Does that make sense?"

"Yes, it does, although I tend to feel the opposite way. I've often felt smothered by my family, and the Indian community as a whole, as we are a close-knit group. Out here I can enjoy the space, the ability to be on my own, and just, well, feel alive."

Thabiti tentatively placed an arm around Marina's shoulder. She leant into him and asked, "Have we failed here?"

Once more Thabiti weighed Marina's words before answering. "No, I don't think so. In fact, your ability to ensure the lodge ran smoothly, despite being in the middle of a murder investigation, was amazing.

"Robert and Vivian had made their plans long before they arrived here, and if they hadn't been able to use this lodge, they'd have found another location and still killed Nina. It's like a game of chess and we were only the pawns."

"What happens when a pawn reaches the far end of a chessboard?"

"It turns into another piece, like a queen, rook or knight."

Marina sighed. "Do you think Mama Rose is like that? Moving across the board without being noticed until she suddenly appears, like a new queen, with the knowledge and insight to solve a case?"

"Poor her, she didn't look like a queen last night, did she? She looked drained, and for the first time I thought she looked her age."

"It's hardly surprising. She and Craig have been together so long. I do hope she's not too lost without him."

Thabiti felt Marina's shoulders shudder as she began to cry. Without thinking, he turned and hugged her to him. Her tears turned to sobs and for several minutes he just held her with his head resting on the top of hers. She smelt faintly of oranges.

Marina's shoulders became still, and she lifted her head and looked at Thabiti with large watery eyes. Her lips were pink and moist and instinctively he leaned down and kissed them. He felt her respond and reach up towards him, opening her mouth and seeking his tongue with hers.

"Oh at last," remarked Pearl as she stepped onto the viewing platform. "I hate to interrupt, but time is getting on and I know how important your meeting with Stella MacDonald is, Marina."

Marina tried to step back, out of their embrace, but Thabiti held her to him and kissed the top of her head. She relaxed against his chest and murmured, "Time to rejoin the real world."

Thabiti parked his white Prado outside Dormans coffee shop. The drive back from Borana had been subdued. Nobody appeared willing to talk, so Thabiti had played his mother's Moipei Sisters CD.

He had driven steadily through the Ngare Ndare forest, and they had stopped to watch a group of five elephants pulling at the branches of wild olive trees at the edge of a clearing beside the road.

They sat down at the large wooden table on Dormans' paved courtyard, opposite the entrance. They had just ordered their drinks when a giggling and smiling Chloe entered, holding hands with a handsome dark-haired man.

Was this the problematic Dan? Nobody had confided in Thabiti, but he had caught snippets of conversation from which he understood that all was not well between Chloe and her husband. But here they were, like two young lovebirds.

Chloe saw them, whispered something in Dan's ear and walked across to join them. Dan sat down at a corner table.

"Are you finished at Borana?" Chloe asked as she shuffled onto the bench next to Marina.

"In the end they couldn't get rid of us quickly enough," replied Thabiti as he fiddled with the menu.

Pearl spoke up. "I think it might be for the best. It's clear you don't enjoy that kind of work, Thabiti, and whilst you're very good at it, Marina, I think it is a waste of your talents."

Marina stared glumly at the table top. "We'll have to see what Stella MacDonald thinks of my talents, and if I am suitable to work at one of her organisation's camps."

"Oh, come here," said Chloe, and gave Marina a hug. As they pulled apart, Marina whispered something to Chloe.

Thabiti couldn't hear everything, but caught the words, "Happy" and "Dan" and "OK."

Chloe whispered back and smiled at Marina.

Pearl leant towards Thabiti and murmured, "Chloe and Dan have been visiting a counsellor to try to get their marriage back on track, and I think it's working."

Thabiti turned to his sister in surprise, "How do you know that?"

Pearl shrugged. "It's one of my new skills, learning to blend in, and to listen and observe rather than always seeking to be the centre of attention. It's actually far more satisfying, and oh, the things I've seen and heard."

"Do you think that is why Mama Rose is so good at solving murder cases?"

"I expect so," said Pearl, as she took her mango smoothie from the waiter and sucked the rich yellow liquid up her straw. She added, "Of course, she has the benefit of years of experience and a better understanding of human nature than I have. But I'm learning."

Thabiti considered his sister. He'd been so worried about her becoming ill again that he hadn't actually noticed the positive change in her. It was as if she had matured years in only a few weeks. He was relieved, and grateful, as he also realised she was eating and drinking again.

Chloe stood and said, "I must get back to Dan. Good luck, Marina."

Thabiti leaned across the table towards Marina and said, "She looked happy."

Marina smiled and replied, "Yes, she and Dan are … starting to understand each other better. She's so pleased, and I do hope it continues. But it's not easy when Dan is away so much, as he retreats inside his head where all sorts of demons lurk."

Pearl finished her smoothie and announced, "I'm going to visit on old friend. I'll make my own way home."

What old friend? Thabiti wondered.

CHAPTER SIXTY-ONE

Thabiti watched Pearl leave Dormans as another lady arrived, someone Pearl would once have described as 'letting herself go'. She had curly hair, with wisps of grey, and she peered around the courtyard through round glasses.

She approached their table and queried, "It's Marina, isn't it?"

"Yes," Marina replied, pushing back the heavy bench and standing to greet the new arrival. She looked at Thabiti and, with a slight inclination of her head, indicated that he should move over.

Instead he stood, and with his hands in his pockets, said, "If you're OK, I'll go to the bank."

Marina nodded, and she and Stella sat down.

Thabiti looked up and down the dusty street, but there was no sign of Pearl. He wandered past the tall concrete casino building and approached Barclays Bank, where he waited in line to use the cash machine.

As he returned to Dormans, he bought a newspaper from a street seller and settled down at the far end of the long wooden table to read it. He also ordered a coffee.

Five or ten minutes later, he wasn't sure how long he had been sitting there, Stella and Marina stood and shook hands. As Stella left, he shuffled up the bench and joined Marina. He retrieved his coffee and asked, "So how did that go? Did she offer you a position?"

Marina bit her lip and answered, "Yes, at the camp Chris told us about in Turkana. The one with all the refugees from Somalia and Ethiopia. But it sounds really tough. I think I'll enjoy helping to distribute food and aid, and I'll also be teaching some of the younger children."

Marina twisted her hands on top of the table and continued, "But part of my role is walking around and inspecting the camp to make sure that nobody is dying, or is badly injured or has been abandoned. Apparently, it's really difficult to distribute the aid evenly and fairly, and some families, especially those with a single parent who is ill or weak, or with elderly grandparents, often miss out."

Thabiti reached across and took one of her hands, "So are you going to accept it?"

She looked up at him and said, "I'm not sure. What do you think?"

He held her gaze. He knew she desperately wanted to prove herself, and to be acknowledged and respected by others. He'd witnessed how her extended family had treated her at the Rhino Charge the previous month.

It was as if being a woman, her only role was as a wife. And because she was refusing to comply with custom, and marry a man of her father's choice, she was only fit to do the bidding of other family members and look after their children.

Thabiti said, "I think you should give it a go, and if it doesn't work out, then at least you know you've tried. Otherwise I think you'll always regret not seizing the opportunity."

Marina smiled faintly and replied, "Thank you. I will."

"Marina," an elderly male voice cried. "There you are. We've been looking all over for you."

Marina pulled back quickly and stood, knocking against the heavy wooden bench. She grabbed hold of the table to steady herself and exclaimed, "Baba, what are you doing here?"

Marina's father was an elderly Indian man who walked with a slight stoop. He explained, "Your mother and I came to Nanyuki to talk to you."

An Indian woman, in a bright red and blue sari, stepped out from behind Marina's father and smiled kindly at them.

Marina extracted herself and hugged her mother. "It's lovely to see you."

Marina's mother giggled. "This is quite an adventure, isn't it? I was so surprised when your father announced we were driving to Nanyuki to find you." She looked serious and held Marina by the shoulders. "He's been very worried, you know, and fretting that we hadn't heard from you and that you were lying dead in a ditch."

Marina pushed the heavy bench out and invited her parents to sit down. Thabiti shuffled along his bench and wondered whether he should leave or move to the far end of the table.

"It's Thabiti, isn't it?" Marina's father asked as he sat down and extended his hand towards Thabiti. Nervously, Thabiti shook it.

Marina blurted, "I'm so sorry I didn't call. We were really busy and ... well I just wasn't sure what to say."

Marina's father tapped his fingers on the table. "I was annoyed with you, daughter, and upset that you ran away to Nanyuki and refused to meet Manu. He's a nice Indian boy and ..."

"Uttamer," chided Marina's mother in a soft voice, but her husband must have noted the steely edge as he pressed his lips together and leaned back. "We promised not to talk about that. I've explained to you that Marina is a modern woman and does not want us to arrange a husband for her. Besides, she has this lovely young man looking after her."

Thabiti felt his mouth open and shut like a wooden puppet as everyone looked at him.

"You're right, Gita." Marina's father bowed his head in her direction. "I'm sorry."

There was an uncomfortable silence, and then Marina's mother asked in a falsely bright voice, "So what have you both been doing?"

"We're been managing a new lodge on Borana Conservancy."

"That sounds fun," her mother replied.

"Not really," said Marina glumly as she rested her chin in her hands on the table. "One of the guests died."

"Why? What did you do?" her father asked sharply.

"I, we, didn't do anything. We were just the pawns in a game of chess. A husband and his," she paused and shrugged, "Lover, killed his wife."

"How awful, my dear," said Marina's mother, pulling Marina to her.

Thabiti thought that Marina had been hugged a lot this morning. He felt uncomfortable until he remembered their embrace at the lodge and then he felt the blood rise to his face.

"Thabiti, are you OK?" asked Marina.

"Fine," he stammered. He looked at Marina's mother and then back at the table as he said, "But Marina's been offered another position. A very interesting job."

"Oh, yes?" enquired her father.

"It's not actually paid work," admitted Marina. "But I have been offered a voluntary position, by an international charity, to work in their base at Kakuma Refugee Camp."

Her mother clasped her hands and cried, "But won't that be dangerous?"

"It will certainly be tough," her father announced. "We send supplies up twice a month and I once made the long trip north. All that poverty and despair. It really upset me."

"So are you going to accept the position?" her mother asked.

"I think so. Thabiti suggested that I at least try it, and if it's not for me, well, then I know and can look for something else to do."

"Or get …" Marina's father started, but hastily stopped when his wife glared at him.

"That's a very sensible suggestion," agreed Marina's mother.

"Yes," muttered her father. "But make sure you look after yourself."

Marina's mother asked, "Are you going as well, Thabiti?"

"Oh, no. I have things to do in Nanyuki. Maybe later."

He looked at Marina who raised her eyebrows.

"Well, you never know," he admitted.

CHAPTER SIXTY-TWO

Pearl walked out of Dormans and looked around

She had surprised herself by announcing that she was going to visit an old friend and even more so that it was blind Mr Kariuki that she wanted to see. She presumed he was still in the Cottage Hospital.

She crossed over Kenyatta Avenue, the main road running through Nanyuki, and the two side streets which ran parallel with it and entered a small arcade of shops located on the ground floor of a three-storey concrete building.

She wanted to take Mr Kariuki a present, but what would he like? There was no point buying him a book since he wouldn't be able to read it.

She stopped as she heard music from one of the small stores. Inside the narrow shop was a glass display cabinet containing various electrical devices, including a CD Walkman. Perhaps that was something Mr Kariuki would find useful.

She wandered towards the back of the shop and scanned the display of CD covers. There was one with the Moipei Sisters. Everyone seemed to be talking about the singing sisters from Nairobi, and she had found the music pleasant enough on the journey back from Borana.

She picked up the CD and began to look through a plastic basket containing CDs of books. She found one with an illustrated African scene on the front.

Turning it over, she discovered it was a recording of a book written by a vet living near Nakuru and was about his experiences when setting up his practice in Kenya. That was something Mr Kariuki might find interesting.

She left the shop with the personal CD player, headphones, and the two CDs, and flagged down a boda boda on the street outside.

At the Cottage Hospital she asked a nurse, "Where can I find Mr Kariuki?"

"He's enjoying some fresh air out in the garden."

Pearl found him at the same bench she had shared with him just over a month before, beside the trickling Nanyuki River. "May I join you?" she asked.

"Why, it's Aisha Onyango's daughter. Ruby, isn't it?"

"It's Pearl, Mr Kariuki."

"Of course it is. Sit down next to me and give me your hand."

She sat on the bench, placed her package beside her, and put her hand in Mr Kariuki's outstretched one.

"There is strength and resolve here," he commented. "And also determination and ..." He looked at her with his cloudy unseeing eyes. "Are you about to embark on a journey?"

"Yes," she gasped. "But how do you know?"

"This is not just a physical one, it is a journey of your soul, and you will face many challenges along your way. But I am glad you have made your decision. You shall be a warrior, but don't forget you also have the ability to be a healer."

He let go of her hand and turned his face in the direction of Mount Kenya. He sighed and opened his arms. "And never forget to embrace the strength of the mountain."

Pearl picked up her package and removed the CD player. She reached up for one of Mr Kariuki's hands and said, "I have something which I hope you will enjoy."

He clasped hold of the CD player and felt it with his other hand. He pushed down a button, and the front popped open.

"It's a personal CD player. Let me show you how it works." She removed the music CD, placed it in his hand and guided it into the player. Then she pressed his hand down to close the compartment.

"Just a minute, you need to listen to it through headphones." She placed the headphones she had just bought over his ears, connected them to the CD player and pressed play.

Mr Kariuki laughed in delight.

She pressed the stop button.

"This is wondrous," he exclaimed. "I can hear the mountain sing to me through the girls' voices."

Pearl smiled and said, "And if you get fed up with the music, the other CD is a spoken book. It's written by a vet about his experience of working in Kenya."

"Bwana Cran?" asked the old man.

Rose looked at the CD cover. "Yes, do you know him?"

"A great man, though small in stature. He has helped many friends with the various troubles they've had with their cattle and dogs. I shall enjoy myself."

Pearl pressed play again, squeezed Mr Kariuki's hand, and left him on the bench.

CHAPTER SIXTY-THREE

C hris drove Rose and Heather to St George's church on Saturday morning in Rose's battered Land Rover Defender. Parked cars lined the approach road.

"It looks like a good turnout for Dad," observed Chris.

"It certainly does, and the car park must be full. I do hope they've saved us a space," Rose fretted.

Chris turned into the car park and spotted an empty parking space, with a reserved sign leaning against a wooden chair, to the left of the church entrance. It was a modest stone church which had replaced the original wooden one built in 1927.

Rose stood on the church's threshold as she heard the Moipei Sisters begin to sing. The last time she had walked down the aisle of a church, before a packed congregation, had been over forty years ago when she and Craig had married in St. Mary's Church in Nakuru.

She registered many faces, all turned towards her, as she walked steadily towards the front of the church flanked by Chris and Heather. There were farmers, not only from Laikipia but from as far afield as Eldoret and Narok, near the Maasai Mara.

Most of the local polo and horse show community appeared to be present, and many more had travelled from Gilgil and Nairobi. And she recognised a group of African workers from the last farm Craig had managed outside Timau, who were huddled together on the right-hand side of the church.

Rose, Chris and Heather took their places in the front pew as the Bishop of Marsabit, who had agreed to make a special visit to lead the memorial service, began the ceremony with the words, "We are gathered here today to celebrate the life of one of our own, Craig Michael Hardie."

Heather stood on the stone step, leading into the choir stalls. She faced the congregation and read Psalm 23.

> *"The Lord is my Shepherd; I shall not*
> *want.*
> *He maketh me to lie down in green*
> *pastures: He leadeth me beside the*
> *still waters.*
> *He restoreth my soul: He leadeth me*
> *in the paths of righteousness for*
> *His name's sake.*
> *Yea, though I walk through the valley*
> *of the shadow of death, I will fear*
> *no evil: for Thou art with me; Thy*
> *rod and Thy staff, they*
> *comfort me.*
> *Thou preparest a table before me in the*
> *presence of mine enemies: Thou*
> *anointest my head with oil; my*
> *cup runneth over.*
> *Surely goodness and mercy shall*
> *follow me all the days of my life:*

and I will dwell in the house of the
Lord forever."

Chris had chosen his own reading. He told the packed church, "I wish to remember my father's life rather than mourn his death and so I have chosen to read, 'I Thank Thee God, That I Have Lived,' by Elizabeth Craven."

"I thank you, God, that I have lived
In this great world and known its many joys;
The song of birds, the strong, sweet smell of hay,
And cooling breezes in the secret dusk,
The flaming sunsets at the close of day,
Hills, and the lonely, heather-covered moors,
Music at night, and moonlight on the sea,
The beat of waves upon the rocky shore
And wild, white spray, flung high in ecstasy;
The faithful eyes of dogs, and treasured books,
The love of kin and fellowship of friends,
And all that makes life dear and beautiful.
I thank you, too, that there has come to me
A little sorrow and, sometimes, defeat,
A little heartache and the loneliness
That comes with parting, and the word
'Goodbye',
Dawn breaking after dreary hours of pain,

When I discovered that night's gloom must
yield
And morning light break through to me again.
Because of these and other blessings poured
Unasked upon my wondering head,
Because I know that there is yet to come
An even richer and more glorious life,
And most of all, because Your only Son
Once sacrificed life's loveliness for me,
I thank you, God, that I have lived."

Rose laughed and cried through Dickie Chambers' eulogy, and she was relieved that his uplifting words, and the amused response of the congregation, raised the spirits inside the church.

It began to feel like a celebration of Craig's life, rather than a memorial of his death. She was thankful, as she knew Craig had wanted a jolly good party to mark his departure.

But when the Moipei Sisters ended the service by singing 'My Land is Kenya' she heard many sobs and the opening of bags as people searched for tissues and hankies to mop their eyes. A number of the men blew their noses.

Finally, the bishop stood in front of the congregation and announced, "Rose, Heather and Chris would like to invite you all to Cape Chestnut for lunch, and to raise a glass, or two, in celebration of Craig's life."

He approached Rose, clasped her hands in his and said, "It's wonderful to see so many people here. And I know how well Craig was liked and respected in the community."

Rose replied, "Thank you. It was a very moving service. Will you join us for lunch?"

"For a short time, thank you, and then I will be visiting patients in the Cottage Hospital and some of those who are now living in the Louise Decker Centre."

The party already appeared to be in full swing as Rose walked through the wooden gate into the garden at the Cape Chestnut restaurant.

She was greeted by a cluster of farmers. "A very fitting send-off," one of them said.

"Thank you for coming so far. Craig would have appreciated it," Rose responded.

Dickie Chambers hovered by the steps to the restaurant veranda. "I hope my eulogy wasn't too long, but there are so many stories, it was difficult to pick just a few."

She touched his arm. "Thank you, Dickie, it was perfect. And so wonderful to remember some of the antics Craig got up to. I'd forgotten many of the stories and his narrow escapes, and I never knew that he was involved in hanging Sybil's underwear from the polo goal posts."

A smiling Chloe approached Rose and handed her a glass of prosecco. "I thought you might need this."

"Oh thank you," Rose replied. "And I think I need some air and a moment to breathe."

Chloe escorted her through the milling crowd towards the large Cape Chestnut tree.

Rose noticed a glow to Chloe's skin and enquired, "Something's changed. Have you and Dan sorted yourselves out?"

Chloe smiled, "We're getting there. I think it may be a bumpy journey, but I feel that for now, at least, we are moving together in the right direction."

Commissioner Akida, Sam and Constable Wachira stood beside the trunk of the Cape Chestnut tree.

"A fabulous turnout for Bwana Craig," greeted the commissioner. "And there are some faces here I haven't seen for decades. Not since I was a young sergeant." He sipped his beer and leant forward, saying, "We have processed Robert Scott Watson and Vivian Scott, but they are to be returned to the UK and prosecuted by the Thames Valley Police."

"And are you happy with that?" Rose asked.

"Extremely. It would be a high-profile case with the potential for bribery and delay. Frankly, I am relieved to hand it over to authorities in the UK so we can return to our quiet lives in Nanyuki."

"They haven't been that quiet recently," mused Sam.

"That is true, and one of the reasons I would like to put forward Constable Wachira for the upcoming sergeant's exams. Her report into the Nina Scott Watson case was clear, concise and comprehensive. Whilst it was Mama Rose who joined the pieces together, I believe Constable Wachira did some excellent investigative work."

"Aren't I a bit young to be a sergeant?" asked Constable Wachira. "And what about Constables Adan and Ngetich. I know they are expecting to be put forward this year."

The commissioner drew his lips together before saying, "Adan is lazy and Ngetich is more interested in lining her own pockets with traffic fines than actually making the roads a safer place. I need a sergeant with initiative who I can rely on to do the right thing."

"That's a great idea," said Sam, encircling the constable's small, athletic shoulders with his large, muscular arm.

"I agree," said Rose. "And what about you, Sam?"

The large man scratched his chin. "I leave tomorrow for an undercover operation in

Tsavo. But for the first time, I'm not excited about going. In fact, I'd rather stay in Nanyuki and solve some more crimes with you, Mama Rose." He grinned.

"Please, I really have had enough of death and murder."

As if remembering why they were there, they all stood in respectful silence. Rose smiled and said, "But I doubt the status quo will last for long. So for now I shall enjoy being reunited with my family and friends."

Sam raised his glass and echoed, "Family and friends." The commissioner, Constable Wachira and Chloe followed his lead.

"I think we should get back to the party," Chloe suggested.

Rose nodded. "Yes, you're right."

They walked back and spotted Thabiti and Pearl standing beside the raised wooden veranda.

Pearl greeted Rose. "Wonderful service. Craig …"

There was a commotion above them and a shout from the restaurant proprietor. "This is a private party. And it's a funeral, so please show some respect."

"I've got every right to be here and pay my respects to Mr Hardie." An African man stood indignantly above them holding a plate piled with food. He swayed unsteadily on his feet.

"You're a disgrace. It's not even noon and you're already drunk."

"I've just had a few drinks to wish Bwana Hardie safari njema."

"I'm afraid I'm going to have to ask you to leave."

The crowd parted as the restaurant proprietor led the African man, who wore a good quality, but worn, pinstripe suit, towards the gate.

As he reached Rose, he beamed, "Thabiti, Pearl, there you are. Please, can you ask this woman to let go of me?"

The proprietor looked at Thabiti with raised eyebrows and asked, "Do you know this man?"

Thabiti kicked at the dusty ground and muttered, "Yes, he's my father."

Mama Rose just wants peace and tranquility to mourn Craig's death, but when a woman collapses and dies in her arms, she's shaken to the core.

She joins an endangered zebra expedition, but alarms bells start ringing when a second woman mysteriously dies in her care.

Buy *Grevy Danger* and ensure that justice is delivered today!

I do hope you've enjoyed Jackal & Hide.

Writing the scenes with Rose, Craig and Chris was very emotional and I was crying as I wrote about Craig's death, and the scattering of his ashes. I've written a bonus scene from Craig's point of view, when Chris and he were in the hospital ward. It discusses their relationship, and that which they both have with Rose.

If you would like to read it please visit www.bit.ly/JHBonus

For more information visit VictoriaTait.com

CPSIA information can be obtained
at www.ICGtesting.com
Printed in the USA
BVHW031937210123
656727BV00003B/732